The Road to Love

Maxine Sullivan

OPAL BAY

Book 1

MAXINE SULLIVAN

ISBN978-0-6456330-0-9

Chapter One

OPAL BAY
Turn Right 1 kilometre

Eden Beresford noted the "Opal Bay" sign as she kept the car chugging north along the highway. To the left of her was the Australian countryside, and way over to the right through a forested area, the Pacific Ocean meandered along the coastline.

She'd meant to meander too, but her

cousin's car had been running rough for the last hour. Now she wasn't sure whether to take the turn coming up and see if she could find someone to look at it or to forge on ahead. Stopping would mean a delay in getting to Port Macquarie by dinnertime. Not that it really mattered. She'd given herself a week to travel to Brisbane and see something of the east coast of Australia while she was visiting here from Perth.

So far, working with her aunt and uncle in their Sydney office these last three months hadn't been as "freeing" as she'd hoped. It had been an incredibly busy time, with business brisk until the end of the year when Christmas had been a welcome break. Sydney was a stunningly beautiful city all right, and her relatives were very nice people who had generously opened their home to them. Yet she'd still felt restless and so had Danny.

Somehow she just hadn't "connected" with anyone or anything on an emotional level. It was disheartening. Or maybe she'd just had her hopes too high. She shouldn't expect a different place and new people to heal the heartache inside her.

Still, she wasn't ready to go back home just yet. The next few weeks were time-out for her and Danny before they returned home to Western Australia and tried to pick up the threads of their old life.

Thunk!

Her eight-year-old son lifted his eyes off the handheld game he was playing. "Mum, what's that noise?"

She glanced down at the blonde, blue-eyed boy on the passenger seat beside her. Everybody said he was the image of her and for that she was grateful. His father certainly didn't deserve any credit for the beautiful child they'd made.

"What noise?" she said, pretending she hadn't heard it.

Thunk!

"*That* noise."

"I think it's a stone," she told him, trying to act casually. "It must have flicked up in the engine, that's all."

"Oh." A pause. "Are we going to break down?"

Break down? God, over a year ago she'd come home early to discover Martin in bed with his lover. After the subsequent divorce, having her car break down on her was nothing. She could handle anything after that.

"We'll be fine, Danny."

Thunk!

Well, okay, so that was a big thunk. Maybe she was fooling herself that she wouldn't have to stop somewhere and get the car looked at sooner rather than later. Not only was Port Macquarie still a bit of a distance away, but it was summer-hot outside the air-conditioned car, and she didn't want them breaking down under the unrelenting sun. If she could just make it to this Opal Bay, then they'd at least be able to take refuge in the shade while the car was being fixed. She wished now that she'd insisted on a hire car instead of listening to her aunt.

You'd be doing us a favour if you used Brad's car while he's traipsing around Europe. It's only a year old. You'll have no problems with it.

"I guess we should get someone to look it over anyway." With a sense of relief, she saw the turn-off ramp coming up ahead. "We'll stop off at the next town."

"Op..al Bay," Danny said, reading the sign out loud.

"Opal, honey," she corrected him, just so he knew.

"Opal," he repeated it the correct way. "Hey, do you think we can go swimming?"

She'd tried to make this trip up the coast an adventure but there were other priorities right now. "I'm not sure. Let's wait until we get there, okay?"

At the end of the ramp, she turned right onto a single-lane road that began to wind a little, and soon the forest on both sides surrounded them. Mentally she kept her fingers crossed that they would make it. Further along, another sign said that Opal Bay was five kilometres away, population two thousand.

As if to keep her on her toes, the car missed a beat. She swallowed. Five kilometres seemed an awfully long way away. And heck, with a population of two thousand people she'd have expected to see at least one other car on this road by now. She sighed. Perhaps they were all inside and out of the sun. Or perhaps they were more likely to be frolicking in the bay. A good frolic sounded just the ticket right now. She wished.

Another kilometre further along, the road straightened ahead and just as she thought that the car would do the right thing, the engine slowed down then cut out altogether. She only had enough time to guide the car to the side of the road before it stopped dead, leaving part of their tail end sticking out a little.

"Damn."

Danny giggled. "You swore!"

She tried to smile and failed. "Sorry, hon, but this is an exceptional circumstance."

His forehead creased. "What's an exceptional circumstance?"

"It means breaking down on a deserted road with our butt sticking out," she said wryly. It was either that or start balling like a cry-baby. This was an adventure she didn't need today. It had been difficult enough getting away from her aunt and uncle this morning, not to mention her mother phoning from Perth to plead with her to fly to Brisbane instead of driving.

"You're funny, Mum."

Eden blinked as she looked at her son. It was good to see him smiling again. He hadn't done much of that this past year. Of course, neither had she. "I'm glad you think so, buster."

Pushing open the driver's door, she slipped off the seat to check how far they were on the road, thankful this hadn't happened nearer the bend. The heat hit her like an oven, the breeze from the ocean having turned hot even this small distance inland, but right now she was more interested in the vehicle. They weren't sticking out a lot, but enough to concern her that some inattentive driver may come at them too fast and smash into them.

She looked around at the countryside, then stuck her head back inside the car. "Honey, it's going to swelter in here soon. How about we go sit under one of the trees by the side of the road and I'll call road service." Hopefully, there was such a thing around here. *Perhaps I should have stayed on the highway. Then at least other cars may have stopped to offer some assistance.* Of course, hindsight is a wonderful thing.

"Will someone come?"

"Of course, they will," she said, instilling confidence in her voice. She moved some boxes around on the back seat and grabbed a blanket, grateful now that her uncle had thought to put some bottled water in the car. There was more than enough to quench their thirst until they were rescued.

Rescued?

She almost laughed then. How the hell did one need rescuing not far from a major regional town like Port Macquarie, and even now she was only a few kilometres from the ocean? If it hadn't been for this eternal January heat, she wouldn't be so worried. They could have walked into the town if it had been cooler, though she wouldn't have liked to leave all her luggage in the car.

She led Danny a safe distance away to one of the gum trees and set them up there, then looked up the local garage on her mobile phone, thankful there was one, and that the battery lasted until she finished the conversation. She was soon talking to someone at Ridgeway's Garage in Opal Bay.

A young-sounding teenager answered, and she quickly told him the problem.

"Granddad's out fixing someone's car but I'll give him a message when he gets back."

That could be ages. "Can anyone else help?"

"My Dad can."

"Good. Tell him to come as soon as possible please." She mentally dropped the age of the young man. He sounded younger than a teenager now.

"Yeah, okay. I'll tell him as soon as he gets back."

Dismay filled her. "He's not there?"

"No."

She held onto her patience. It wasn't the child's fault that his family had left him in charge, but she was tired from driving all morning, tired from having wrapped up everything in her old life, tired from an incredibly selfish ex-husband who wouldn't willingly give a cent to her or his son. Yeah, she needed this right now like a hole in the head.

It would match the hole in her heart.

"Honey, whoever gets back first please ask them to come out and get me. Thanks." She disconnected the call while she still had some battery power left in the phone. Then she glanced down at her son. "We might have to wait a while."

"That's okay, Mum. We can pretend we're having a picnic."

She groaned inwardly, then as quickly took a deep breath. *Right, stop that!* She was here in the gorgeous countryside with her beautiful son and that's all she needed. They were going to have a wonderful trip.

Oh yes, they were.

"Good idea." She went back to the car and

grabbed two bottles of water then plopped down on the rug. It was important to keep up their fluids on a hot day like this. "Here, let's have a drink. And then we'll tuck into the fried chicken," she joked of the imaginary food and he chuckled, the sound music to her ears.

Soon they had wriggled their backs up against the tree trunk and made themselves comfortable while they drank their water. It tasted warm but at least it was somewhat refreshing.

Half an hour later, not one car had passed. Eden had pulled her shoulder-length blonde hair into a ponytail and was fanning them both with a magazine. The crackling sound of the heat filled the forest and the sun tried to scorch their faces through the tree branches above. Sweat plastered her tank top and shorts to her skin now, and for some reason she thought of her mother. No way would Regina

Blake recognise the hot and dusty woman as the same well-groomed daughter she'd raised. Even *she* didn't recognise herself these days. Too much heartache had happened to ever go back to the woman she'd been.

Sure, having an ex who'd taken off with his lover to another city a year ago, then who'd decided to come back and disrupt her and Danny's life again, certainly changed a person. She'd never have taken him back anyway — *never* — but she needn't have worried. He wasn't returning to share their lives, he'd said, but to get his share of the house sale and set up house with his lover. Perth hadn't been big enough for all of them after she'd learned that.

Just then she saw a car approaching from the direction of the highway. "Someone's coming." She breathed with relief, glad to shake off her thoughts.

She scrambled to her feet, squinting to see through the ribbons of heat along the road. At least they could get a ride into town now — and to hell with the luggage.

Danny was on his feet too. "Cool!"

Yet as the car approached, the hairs on the back of Eden's neck lifted when she saw the silver sedan slow down then pull over to the side. There was a man behind the wheel. Just her luck it wasn't a woman. She'd have no difficulty hitching a ride with a female but a male who was physically stronger...

Her heart pounded and she grabbed a stick from the ground. She would be ready for the stranger if need be. She and Danny were alone out here, and one never knew about people. She'd learned that first-hand with Martin. Appearances were deceptive.

"Danny, let me do the talking," she whispered, repositioning herself in front of him. She'd fight to the death to protect her son. She swallowed. Dear God, let's hope it didn't come to that, and the guy was simply being a good Samaritan. Not everyone was a serial killer, she told herself. The sound of the cicadas echoed through the trees, making her feel even more isolated.

The dark-haired man eased his long legs out of his car. Even from this distance, she could tell he was good-looking, but it didn't discount the fact that he was tall and could easily outrun her and Danny.

He started towards them but it was in a laidback way that was pure Australian. Yet she couldn't let herself be deceived merely because the man did full justice to his jeans and shirt. She had to keep in mind that he could be dangerous. She had to be prepared for anything until she was totally sure about him.

He stopped a few feet away. "G'day," he drawled from behind a pair of dark sunglasses.

His greeting might be friendly enough, but it didn't ease her mind one iota. She didn't trust a man who didn't take off his sunglasses. And she wasn't taking off her own sunglasses now either. She didn't want him seeing even a hint of fear in her eyes.

She nodded. "Hello."

"Problem with your car?"

Her hand tightened on the stick – just in case. "What makes you say that?"

There was a moment's pause. "Nobody would park here in the heat unless it was necessary."

"Oh." That made sense.

His eyebrows suddenly drew together. "You *do* realise the ocean's just a few kilometres ahead, don't you?"

"Of course." Did he think she couldn't read or something? She held onto the stick. "We were having a picnic, that's all," she said, playing for time, hoping another car might come along any minute now, just to make her feel safer.

He glanced down at the car rug at their feet, then he looked at Danny, then on to her. "The ants ate all the food, did they?" he drawled.

"How did you guess?" she quipped.

"It was a pretend picnic," Danny suddenly said, moving a little forward and Eden put her hand on his shoulder to keep him at her side.

The man looked at Danny and his features softened. "I see. My son likes to have pretend picnics too."

"You have a son?" Danny asked, and something kicked inside her. Lucky woman to be married to this guy. Physically, anyway. She had no idea of his personality. He could still be the local serial killer for all she knew. She swallowed hard.

The man nodded and smiled. "Yep. His name is Sean. He's probably around your age. That would be nine, right?"

Danny's chest puffed up. "I'm eight but I look nine."

"There you go then, mate. I was almost right."

Danny looked up at his mother. "See, Mum. I'm getting big now."

"Yes, I know." Eden had watched the interchange, releasing a small silent sigh of relief. Something about the guy made her calmer now, yet that was crazy. Just because a man was a father and a husband, didn't make him any less dangerous. Not to mention a set of perfect white teeth when he smiled.

Still, it was time to get down to business. She stepped out from under the gum tree but kept her expression firm. "Look okay, there is a problem with my car. Perhaps you could take a look?"

"What's wrong with it?" he said, in a blank voice that made her question if she'd imagined that awareness between them.

"If I knew that, I'd be a mechanic," she said with a touch of sarcasm, then felt shrewish when she saw him look at her sharply. "Sorry. It's the heat." It's been making a funny noise for the last hour, then it just stopped and I thought it was okay. It's my cousin's car. He lent it to us and I'm not sure if it was there before."

"What sort of noise?"

"It sounded like a thunk."

He scowled. "A *thunk*?"

She nodded. "That's the best way to describe it."

"Where was the noise? The front?"

"Yes."

He turned and strode towards her car and she and Danny followed. She studied him as he popped the bonnet and fiddled under it, seeming to know his way around an engine. The wife in her wanted to tell him to be careful getting grease on his clean shirt, but the woman in her said it wasn't her concern.

He straightened and pushed the bonnet back down. "Looks like you're going to need a tow to the garage." He took his mobile phone out of his pocket and started to turn away. "I'll arrange it."

"I've already called them."

He glanced back. "When?"

"About forty minutes ago, I guess. A child answered and told me he'd pass the message on when his grandfather and father get back," she said, unable to stop the disapproval in her voice. She didn't understand the mentality of some people.

"I see. Well, I'm sure the tow truck will be here soon then. I'll just check anyway." He started using his mobile phone as he took off for his sedan, but she could only hear his muffled tones as he began to speak to someone on the other end. No doubt the child she'd spoken to. She watched as he hung up and began to rummage around in the boot of his car. Then he came towards them with a length of rope in his hands.

"What's that for?" she asked cautiously.

More than cautious, actually.

He looked surprised, then his lips stretched

with one of those white smiles. "This isn't the Wild West, lady. Your car's parked dangerously." He went to the front of her car. "I need to straighten it, so it doesn't get in anyone's way."

Her shoulders relaxed. "Couldn't you just push it?"

"With one hand or two?" he said dryly, and she gave a light chuckle before she could stop herself. Without warning, he seemed to still a moment, then as quickly cleared his throat. "Normally I would push it, but the right front tyre's in a bit of a ditch here." He jerked his head at her car. "Hop in while I bring my car around to the front of yours. Once I've tied the rope, I'll get you to release the brake then put it back on after I straighten you up. The tow truck is on its way." He paused. "Okay?"

She nodded, but she was still wondering

about the way he'd frozen a moment ago. Then Danny fidgeted beside her, and she pushed her thoughts aside. "Danny, you go sit on the blanket and don't move." She didn't want him inside the hot car with her.

And it *was* hot.

Hot as hell, she decided as she slid in behind the steering wheel, then waited for the man to park in front of her. It didn't take long before he was tying the rope between the vehicles, and suddenly she could look at him without worrying he'd catch her out. He really was quite handsome, and the heat did nothing to discount that. He seemed quite at ease with it all.

Unlike her.

It was stupid, but watching him she went over all feminine, feeling self-conscious about her hair damply pulled back in a ponytail and her tank top sticking to her breasts. No one could ever accuse her of being beautiful though she'd often been called pretty when growing up, but right now she felt more like a rag doll than a Barbie.

Soon he'd gone back to his car, and she pushed her thoughts aside and released the brake, allowing her car to move forward. A moment later, his brake lights flashed, and Eden concentrated on what she had to do. She applied her own brakes. Only, nothing happened. She pumped the pedal again, then in desperation reefed on the parking brake... nothing worked... the car wouldn't stop... at least not until it skidded into the back of his sedan with a jolting bump.

"Oh damn!"

Chapter Two

Eden glanced at the man looking at her through his car mirror. She could well imagine what he would be thinking.

He eased his vehicle forward, then got out to inspect the damage. She climbed out of her car too, instructing Danny to stay where he was. She didn't want her son to come near the road, knowing he would if given half a chance.

Then she hurried towards the man. "I don't know what happened. Honestly, I applied the brakes. Twice. I even tried the parking brake —"

He straightened. "Relax. It's not your fault. The car slid on the gravel on the side of the road here." He kicked the powdery dirt with the toe of his shoe. "See. The tyres couldn't get a proper grip, that's all."

Relief rolled through her. "Oh, is *that* what it was? I thought I'd done something wrong." She bent forward to examine the vehicles. "Look, there's just a slight mark on the —" She spun around — and caught him eyeing her bare legs beneath her shorts. "Er... bumper," she finished lamely.

He looked away, as if angry with himself. "It's only a scratch."

"No matter," she said in her best no-nonsense voice. "It'll still have to be repaired."

"Don't worry about it."

"But —"

Suddenly she could hear the rumble of an engine coming from the direction of town.

"Here's the tow truck now," he cut across her thoughts, putting an end to the conversation. He turned and gestured to the driver to pull off the road, then strode away.

She watched him talk to the other man, but her heart was racing like she'd been in a grand prix. Okay, so the man had taken a peek at her legs. Big deal. At least it proved he was a man who liked women.

Not that she cared one way or the other, she told herself, straining her ears but unable to hear what was being said over the sound of the tow truck's engine.

"Mum, look the tow truck's here," Danny

said, suddenly appearing beside her, startling her.

"Danny, I thought I told you to stay under the tree."

"But Mum, I just wanted to tell you it's here." That was his simple reasoning, and she was too darn hot to take him to task further. She let it go.

The stranger went to untie the rope and move his sedan, and the tow truck driver reversed up to the front of her car then hopped down out of the cabin, his work boots carrying a tall, rangy body in faded jeans and a black t-shirt. He looked like he was in his late fifties and must be the grandfather that teenager had been talking about.

He perched his sunglasses on top of his greying head as he came towards her and Danny. "I see you need some help," he said in a kindly manner.

Earlier thoughts of castigating him for

taking so long disappeared now that help was here. "Yes, thank you. We're so glad you're here." She was pleased to see he'd taken off his sunglasses... unlike a certain other man... Still, she'd left hers on.

"My name's Tom Ridgeway."

She smiled. "I'm Eden and this is my son, Danny."

Tom nodded at them both, then indicated the other man. "Grant said you needed a tow back to town."

Grant. So that was the younger man's name. Hmm, she liked it. Not that it mattered, she quickly told herself. He was married, she was divorced.

"I'm not sure what's wrong with it," she told him, "but if you could take it back to your garage and fix it, I'd really appreciate it."

He nodded. "We'll see what we can do." He rotated on his boots. "Son, let's get this car hooked up."

"Sure, Dad."

Eden was startled as Grant deviated towards the back of the tow truck, where the two men began fiddling with chains and the like. He hadn't even looked at her, yet he must have known she'd be a little taken aback to learn he was the tow truck driver's son, especially after what she'd said about them taking so long in getting here. And that meant the child who'd answered the phone was probably Grant's son. It was completely odd, but she'd expected more of this Grant than leaving his young son minding the store.

"Mum, did you hear that? He's that man's dad."

"So it seems," she murmured, irritated at the mild deception, despite knowing he owed her nothing.

"Don't you like him, Mum?"

She glanced down to find her son staring up at her. Danny was a shrewd little boy at times. They both knew he was talking about Grant and not his father. "No, it's not that. I just feel a little silly, that's all."

"Why?"

She smiled. "How about when we get to town, we get an ice cream?"

"Yeah!"

Her distraction worked, and after that her car was already hooked up to the tow truck.

"You two can travel in my car," Grant said, once they'd finished, not looking at all embarrassed about not telling her who he was.

Danny tugged at her hand. "Mum, I want to ride in the tow truck."

The older man spoke before she could. "I

don't mind. Your mother can ride with Grant. It'll be more comfortable for her anyway. She'll be right behind us."

"No, that's fine," Eden said quickly, suddenly not wanting to leave her son alone with a stranger, not to mention being left alone herself with a very attractive stranger in the confines of his car.

"Mum, *please*?"

She looked at the disappointment on Danny's face. Heck, it was only a tow truck ride, after all. And she'd be right behind them. "Okay, honey, you can ride in the truck."

Her son broke into a big smile. "Thanks, Mum!"

They were soon in their respective vehicles and on their way with the air-conditioning turned up high. Grant kept his sunglasses on, and so did she.

The car windows were lightly tinted but it was still very glary outside. And she didn't need to know the colour of his eyes anyway.

"So," she said, once the refreshingly cold breeze had cooled her down. "You're the garage owner's son?"

He kept his eyes on the road. "Yep."

"You should have said."

He shot her a quick sideways look. "Why?"

"Well... because."

"That's a good reason," he drawled.

Clearly, she wasn't going to get an explanation, so she wasn't even going to mention what she thought of him leaving his son alone. "Do you know what's wrong with my car?" she asked, changing to a more immediate problem as they picked up a little speed.

"I have a suspicion."

"And?"

"I'll tell you when I know for sure."

She grimaced as she looked out the side window at the passing trees. He was clearly a man who played his cards close to his chest.

For a while, they drove in silence behind the tow truck.

"Going far?" he finally said, taking her by surprise that he'd spoken at all. No doubt he'd noted her absence of a wedding ring and had to be wondering about her circumstances.

"Yep," she mocked, repeating him earlier.

He shot her a wry look. "Heading anywhere in particular?"

"North." He wasn't the only one who could play this game of short answers, she decided, though it was automatic for her not to give too much information away. He *was* a stranger after all.

He flicked her a glance. "Listen, I'm just trying to make conversation here but —" His voice said he clearly didn't care one way or the other.

"Brisbane. That's where we're heading."

His brow rose. "There. Was that painful?"

She gave a faint smile. "Yep."

He laughed and the low sound shivered along her spine in a pleasurable way.

Then he frowned. "Is the air-con too cold?"

"A... a little. But it doesn't matter. We'll be there soon."

"Actually... we're there right now."

The road followed a bend and there in front of them was the sleepy seaside hamlet of Opal Bay. She gave an exclamation of delight. Surrounded by a hinterland of lush vegetation, the jewel of a town had the Pacific Ocean as a backdrop and was set around a necklace-shaped bay lined by a white sandy beach. She could see where it got its name.

"Oh it's beautiful," she whispered, amazed she could look at anything with wonder anymore. Thank God she hadn't let Martin ruin everything for her.

"It is, isn't it?" the man beside her said, sounding pleased. She couldn't take her eyes off the panoramic view as they drove towards the small coastal town. Then they were on the main street that arrowed towards the blue waters of the bay and fanned out around the small pier. A short distance further and they turned left into Ridgeway's Garage.

A young dark-haired version of Grant came racing out of the office as they alighted from the sedan. He stopped dead when he saw her and gave a shy smile, then smiled at his father. "Hi, Dad."

Grant nodded a greeting. "Sean. Everything quiet around here?"

"Yep." The boy's eyes darted towards Eden. "Except there was a lady —"

"That was me, Sean," Eden said, with a smile. "Hi, I'm Eden."

He looked shy again. "Hi."

The tow truck had rumbled to a stop in front of the office, then Tom put it into gear and noisily reversed back into the workshop area. Eden waved at a beaming Danny sitting up there inside the truck's cabin. She was glad she'd let him ride up there now. Tick one more experience for him.

"Hey Sean, come and help us with this," Tom called out as he opened the door and hopped down from the truck's cabin.

"Sure, Granddad." The kid took off, though his steps slowed as he got closer to Tom helping Danny down from the truck, as if he'd suddenly gone shy again.

He seemed a sweet kid, Eden thought, as she watched Tom introduce the two boys then give instructions that had them running over to a bench where some tools were kept.

"Now wait there until I say so," Tom said, and walked around the back of the truck.

Eden kept her eyes on the boys to make sure they did what they were told, and once satisfied she couldn't keep quiet any longer. She took off her sunglasses and placed them on top of her head then shot Grant Ridgeway a slight look of disgust. "I can't believe you'd leave your son here alone while you're out on the road."

He looked taken aback then his mouth tightened. Like he was in a showdown he placed his own sunglasses on top of his head. "I didn't know I needed your approval."

She ignored the fact that he had the most

gorgeous blue eyes. "But he's too young to be left alone." She wondered if his mother was at work, but in any case, surely the woman didn't approve of this?

"He's usually not left alone for any length of time. Anyway, today was unusual. I had to go into Port Macquarie and Dad was called out on a job at the last minute. It was unavoidable."

Or were they just being cheap? "Maybe if you paid someone to run the office," she began. "Perhaps —"

"Old Bill next door at the barber's keeps an eye out," he cut across her. "He's over here like a shot if someone comes. Nothing gets past him."

"Oh." Well, perhaps that wasn't too bad in such a small community. She was just used to the city.

"And besides," he continued, "it teaches him

responsibility." He glared at her, his blue eyes like steel. "I don't know why I'm bothering explaining this to you anyway. It's none of your bloody business." He stalked away towards the others.

She stared at his back. He was an odd mixture of a man. One minute he seemed to have a softer side, the next he was rearing up at her like a stallion protecting his young. At least she couldn't blame him for that, she thought, following him. She needed to see about her car whether she'd upset Grant or not.

Inside the workshop, Tom made a comment to Grant then the older man approached her, wiping his hands on a rag. She figured he'd lost the toss to speak to her.

"We could be a while here, Eden. Do you want to take a look around town?"

She glanced behind her towards the street.

"Good idea."

"Mum, you said we could get an ice cream, remember?" Danny said, coming up to her with Sean beside him.

She smiled and ruffled her son's hair. "I did too." She glanced at Tom. "Where's the best place for ice cream around here?"

He indicated further along the street. "Sally's Place. Down the road there a bit. You can sit out on the verandah and enjoy the afternoon breeze coming off the bay. Sally's famous for her milkshakes."

"Ooh yum!" Danny exclaimed.

Eden had to smile at her son's enthusiasm. It was wonderful to see. "Sounds good. Thanks for the suggestion." She went to turn, then stopped. "Would you like to come with us, Sean?"

"Oh boy, would I!" he exclaimed, his

shyness disappearing. Then he looked at his grandfather and his shoulders drooped. "Um... I can't," he said, and Eden felt sorry for the kid. Was this another example of Grant's 'responsibility'?

Tom eyed his grandson with a wry smile. "Okay, drop the long face, sonny. You can go."

Sean's eyes lit up. "I can?"

"I'll square it with your father."

"Yippee!"

"Yeah, yippee!" Danny repeated, and Eden couldn't help but smile at Tom, who took some money out of his pocket and went to give it to her. She waved it aside. "Allow me to pay. I'm happy the boys can keep each other company."

He nodded. "That's very nice of you."

They left then and were soon sitting on the deck. Sally knew Sean, of course. She was a pleasant woman who chatted as she served them.

Danny decided on a chocolate milkshake instead of ice cream, and so did Sean. Eden had a vanilla one and decided that Tom was right. The milkshakes were divine.

The boys seemed to have hit it off and the view of the bay was soothing, but she was trying not to worry too much about the car. It was three o'clock now and if they fixed it in an hour or two then she and Danny could be on their way.

If not...

On their return, Sean and Danny raced straight into the office to tell Tom about their milkshakes, while she went straight into the workshop. Grant was working under the bonnet of someone else's car. She was vaguely aware he had pulled on dark blue overalls over his clothes, and with the combination of the grease, the tools, and the workshop, he was looking even more masculine.

She swallowed before speaking. "How did you go then?"

He didn't look up. "We need to get a part brought in."

"Damn."

He lifted his head.

Their eyes locked. Once again, she was taken aback by the blueness of his eyes. Then he looked away and the moment passed, but she couldn't help but wonder if he'd noticed her eyes were green.

And he was married, she reminded herself, certain she wouldn't like such a look to pass between her husband and another woman. Then she remembered Martin. *Her unfaithful husband.* He'd been interested in more than another person's eyes.

"You can't fix it yourself?" she asked, getting back to the matter at hand.

"I could. If I had the part."

Her lips pursed in exasperation as she watched him continue working. "Well, how long will that take?"

"It should be here by tomorrow afternoon."

"What!"

He straightened and looked at her full on again, but there was nothing the least personal in his eyes now. "You in a hurry?" he asked, like it was something unheard of in this neck of the woods. She was beginning to believe that was the truth.

"Well, no. But I might prefer to leave here sooner rather than later."

"You could hire a car, if that's what you want." He was all business now. "Of course, you'd still have to come back from Brisbane and pick up this one. Or have it freighted to Brisbane. If you have the money, that is."

It wasn't really about the money. She had a nice lump sum from her share of the sale of the house now, though she wasn't about to fritter it away. She couldn't let herself be reliant on her mother for too long once she returned to Perth either. Her mother would have them stay with her permanently if she could, but Eden had already refused. She needed her independence more than ever now.

He picked up a screwdriver. "Didn't you say this was your cousin's car? You could get it freighted back to Sydney, then hire a car yourself and continue to Brisbane."

She stared at him. "I'm amazed by your helpfulness all of a sudden," she mused.

He shrugged. "Just trying to help a lady on her way."

Oh, she just bet he was, she thought

watching him stick his head under the bonnet of the car. Then her mind turned to his suggestion. She supposed she *could* get it freighted back to Sydney early. She was going to do that once she'd finished the job in Brisbane and heading back to Perth. Only, that posed a problem right now. A big one. Once she telephoned them in Sydney and told them what had happened, her aunt would fret and would telephone her mother in Perth, and then her mother would fret and her uncle would be assigned to come and get her and Danny. She didn't want that. She didn't want to go back to Sydney, nor worry her mother. She wanted to go to Brisbane. With her son. This was *their* adventure, and no one was going to spoil it for them.

Not even this man in front of her.

"So, there's a hire car service around here?" she asked, just in case she needed to have the car freighted to Brisbane.

Grant shook his head. "You have to go into Port Macquarie for that."

O.K.A.Y... "Is there a cab to get to Port Macquarie then?"

"No. There's a daily bus, but you've missed it."

"So why mention the hire car if I can't get to any place today to hire one?" she asked, about to lose her patience.

He slanted her a sideways look. "It was a thought for tomorrow, that's all."

Her eyes widened. "Tomorrow? You don't think the car will be fixed by then?"

He straightened with a frown this time. "It all depends on when the part gets here."

They were going round and round in circles so much she was going to be dizzy. And right now she knew one thing. She was beginning to feel trapped...

trapped in paradise. Her mother must have known a thing or two by naming her Eden. And Grant was the snake, and his father was offering milkshakes instead of apples.

And she was getting crazier by the minute. Must be the heat.

She took a calming breath. "Looks like we'll have to stay in a motel overnight. You *do* have one of those, don't you?"

He nodded. "Go down the end of the street and turn left. It's around the corner, within easy walking distance."

Clearly that was that then.

"Or there's a pub," he said. "They might have a room and it's probably cheaper."

Tom suddenly appeared at her side. "Forget the pub, Eden," he said, shooting Grant a cross look. "It can get a bit noisy there. The motel is best for you and Danny. It's their busy time of year but they should have a vacancy. If not, you can stay with us for the night. We have a spare bedroom."

"What!" Grant said. "Dad, look —"

"Tom, it's very nice of you," Eden said quickly before Grant choked, "but I'm sure the motel will have a vacancy." Oh, she prayed they did now. If not, she and Danny would sleep in the car. Or on the park bench. Or...

"Look," Tom said, "check with Jake at the motel first. I was speaking to him earlier and he'd said he'd had a couple of late cancellations."

Eden could feel herself breath again, as no doubt so did Grant.

"We can drive you," Tom continued. "You've got too much luggage to walk."

She didn't want to put anyone out further. "No, that's okay. We only need two of the lighter suitcases. I can manage."

Tom waved a dismissive hand. "Go book yourself in and tell Jake I sent you. Grant will bring your luggage as soon as he can."

She darted a look at Grant, whose head was back hovering over the engine. He didn't look up, but she knew the last thing he would want was to be running after a stranger. Or to have them in his home. And of course, then she'd have to meet his wife. The woman might not appreciate strangers in her home.

"Thank you for all your help," she said sincerely, then called to Danny, then nodded at Tom. "See you tomorrow."

It was a short walk to the motel and thank heavens there *was* a vacancy. She really wasn't sure what she would have done if there hadn't been. She would no doubt have had to take up the offer of the spare room. On the other hand, she now suspected Grant would have driven them into Port Macquarie if she'd asked. Yeah, he'd probably have insisted on it, she mused.

It was after five before her luggage was delivered to her room, not by Grant but by the owner of the motel, Jake. Grant must have dropped it off at Reception then left and that was fine with her. No doubt he was eager to take his son and go home to his wife.

Lucky man. At least he had a home to go to. She and Danny had her mother's place back in Perth, but when it came to their own home... their very own sanctuary from the world... they actually had none.

Chapter Three

"Do you want the bad news now or later?" Grant said when she walked into the garage around ten the next morning.

Eden prepared for the worst. Danny had gone to talk to Sean inside the office and there was no sign of Tom. The tow truck was missing too, so she figured the older man had gone out on a job, more's the pity. She'd prefer to deal with Tom Ridgeway rather than Grant. Tom didn't make her feel like she constantly needed to be on guard.

"Just give it to me straight." Was today already shaping up to be the same as yesterday?

"Our supplier can't get the part here until tomorrow."

She shrugged. "Simple. Go to another supplier."

"Our guy handles all the orders in the area. Even if we get it from Sydney, it will still take until tomorrow to get here and then I still have to fix the car."

"You're kidding me, right?"

"No."

"Damn."

Grant's eyes narrowed. "Why? Don't you have enough money to stay the extra night?"

She thrust out her chin. "Is that your way of

asking if I can pay your bill?"

His face hardened. "Not at all."

She expelled a breath. All right, so the man was only trying to help her. "I have enough money to pay my way, thanks."

"Fine." He picked up one of the tools and went back to working on the car in front of him. Not *her* car, she noted, but someone else's car. No, *her* car couldn't be worked on until tomorrow. And clearly, she was of no importance to this man until then.

She stood there, trying to decide what to do. They were cleaning the rooms at the motel and she and Danny would only be in the way right now, but she'd feel better once she confirmed the room for another night, so that would be a priority.

"You should take a walk around the bay while you're here," he said, still working on the engine.

Clearly, he wanted her to go. And it was a

reminder that she was only here temporarily and clearly less than significant to him. And that was exactly how it was supposed to be, and it shouldn't account for the little stab to her heart. She took comfort in the fact that nobody liked to feel they weren't wanted, whether in a minor way with this mechanic, or in a major way with a husband.

"Good idea." She'd dressed in Capri pants and a tank top, already planning on doing exactly that this morning anyway. And she would still do that once they stopped by the motel. She'd grab her sunhat while she was there too.

She saw the two boys chatting away to each other in the office area. "Do you mind if Sean comes with us? I promise I'll look after him."

Grant straightened. "He's grounded for two weeks."

Aah, that explained why Sean hadn't thought

he'd be able to go for ice cream yesterday. She felt sorry for the kid. Spending two weeks of his summer holidays with grown-ups sounded a little harsh.

"Grant," she automatically said, the name sounding strange on her lips, "I know it's none of my business, but it looks to me like he's been very helpful around the place. Surely it wouldn't hurt to let him have some time off today just while we're here? He could go back to be grounded tomorrow once we've gone." The man's blue eyes bored into hers and she shrugged. "I'm just saying."

He paused a moment. "Is this for Sean's sake... or for yours?"

She drew her eyebrows together. "What do you mean?"

"You want my son to keep your son busy so that you don't have to be bothered yourself, right?"

She gasped. "That's not true. I just thought the kid needed a break from..." Words welled up in her throat "...from a heartless father who thinks a child should be like an adult and not a kid."

Surprise flashed in his eyes, then he gave her a bemused smile. "You're very passionate about things, aren't you?"

Was she? Martin hadn't thought so.

"Only for some things," she said, then froze when she saw desire spring into his eyes, her words rearing up in a sexual attraction like a serpent about to strike. She gulped. "I mean..." God, how did she say this without bringing this *thing* further out in the open? Hell, the man was *married* for heaven's sake!

Grant saved the day by spinning away and striding to the office. "Sean, can you come out here for a minute?"

"Sure, Dad." He did as asked with Danny

following more slowly.

"I want you to show Mrs. Beresford and Danny around the place," Grant said, not looking at her. "They want to take a walk around the bay. Do you think you can do that?"

Sean's face lit up. "You betcha!"

"Make sure you stay with Mrs. Beresford. And no going out on the water," he said sternly.

"I won't, Dad."

"You're still grounded after this."

"I know," he said, but his excited voice said he clearly didn't care right then. He and Danny ran for the footpath.

"Wait!" Eden called after them. Somehow, she managed a smile for Grant, warming to him for the way he'd handled the situation. He'd relented without giving in altogether. Maybe he wasn't so bad after all. "Thanks for this."

He gave her a devastating smile that stunned her. "No, thank *you* for caring about my son."

She stared. She couldn't help it. That smile sent her pulse skipping. She'd thought he was handsome before but now there was an extra dimension to his looks. This man could be a danger to a woman in more ways than one. It was just as well that he was married. And she wasn't interested anyway.

She edged towards the sunshine outside. "Er... I'd better go."

The telephone rang and his smile slid away as he headed for the office, leaving her to hurry after the boys on unsteady knees. She didn't think he had any idea how much kick had been in that smile. She felt almost punch-drunk, like it was going to follow her around for a long time to come. And perhaps on some Perth winter nights she might even drag it out and remember.

And she was getting too crazy again, she told herself as she hurried out of the garage. It was this place doing this to her and nothing more. There was just something about being here that heightened her senses and made everything seem out of the ordinary.

The boys hadn't waited for her and had started along the main street towards the bay. She'd almost caught up to them when she heard them talking.

"Whatcha grounded for?" she heard Danny ask.

Sean gave a big sigh. "Me and Jamie took one of the rowboats out on the bay and almost drowned. Dad really went crazy."

"Wow!"

Sean shrugged. "It was nothin'."

Eden inhaled sharply. No wonder Sean had

been grounded for two weeks. And she'd taken Grant to task for disciplining his son so harshly. She'd have done exactly the same. More. She'd have grounded Danny for a month! No, make that a year.

"Is Jamie your best friend?"

"Yeah."

"I had to leave my best friend back in Perth."

Her mind centered on her son, and the sadness in his voice made her heart lurch with anxiety. *Oh, God.* Damn Martin for causing such upheaval in their lives. *Damn him. Damn him. Damn him.* If it wasn't for him, they would all be back in Perth together – a married couple and their child — a family together. That's the way it was supposed to be.

"Jamie and me are best buddies."

Sean's voice drew her attention back to the

boys in front of her.

"What's your best friend's name?" he continued.

"Pete."

"Do you miss him?"

Something inside went tight as she waited to hear the answer. She'd felt guilty dragging Danny away from his friend.

"Sometimes I miss him," he said, "but I really like being here with my mum too."

A little valve of pressure unwound inside her. Thank you, Lord!

She saw Danny tilt his head at Sean. "Where's your mum? Does she live with you?"

"She's dead."

"Oh," Danny said. He seemed to hesitate. "That's too bad."

"Yeah. Is your Dad dead?" Sean asked.

"No. He left to go live with someone else. Mum's divorced."

Eden fumbled to think as the shock of Sean's mother being dead took precedence over hearing Danny talk so matter-of-factly about his own situation. If Sean didn't have a mother, then that meant Grant didn't have a wife.

Her heart skipped a beat, *not* because Grant was free to pursue a relationship with any woman he wanted, but because he *wasn't* being unfaithful to his wife by being attracted to *her*, even unwillingly and even if he'd never admit it. And that meant he *wasn't* the least bit like Martin, who'd been attracted to someone else and taken that person as his lover in spite of being married. So, there *were* some good, decent men left in the world.

Not that she was seriously interested in Grant like that, but it did make her feel better about everything now. And really, the main thing here was that Sean didn't have a mother. Poor kid.

"Hey, you two, wait for me," she said, then caught up with them in a couple of steps. "I need to stop at the motel first."

Thankfully, Jake confirmed the room was available for another night. Then the rest of the walk along the main street was pleasant, with people greeting them, and a couple of store owners waving to Sean as they passed by. The town had a homely feel, yet it clearly catered for holidaymakers, though not in a big way like some of the touristy towns. She could imagine that after staying here on holiday, families would come back year after year, in both summer and winter. It was that sort of place.

Before they hit the beach, Eden stopped to buy sunscreen, then applied it to the boys' skin not covered by their shorts and t-shirts, and then did the same for herself. It wasn't hot yet, but she didn't want any of them getting burned, and being near the water tended to make a person forget just how much power the sun could pack.

On the sand, they kicked off their sandals and headed for the water that was casually lapping the beach. The boys skylarked in the shallows as they got rid of some pent-up energy, and she laughed, pleased to see them having fun. Then they settled down and took a walk along the beach.

"That's my house over there." Sean pointed in the direction of some houses across the bay.

Perfectly-positioned, it was a big house that no doubt had a magnificent view of the crystal-clear water. The wide deck was clearly meant to be lazed around on while watching the children play in the large backyard leading down to the beach.

"It's great," Danny said, the envy in his voice resounding inside Eden. It did look great.

"I live there with my dad and my granddad and my Aunt Carly and Zoe. Uncle Ryan and Uncle Jared have their own places."

"Do you like it?"

"Yeah. Me and my dad like living near the water. We didn't always."

So, Sean and Grant hadn't always lived in Opal Bay. Now *that* was a surprise, considering how at home they appeared to be. She wondered where they had lived before. And what had happened to Grant's late wife?

Forget it.

She should be minding her own business.

The stroll around the bay was sheer delight. There were families playing with their children, couples stretched out on the white sand soaking up some sun, older people fishing from different vantage points along the small pier or throwing a line in the water from their rowboats bobbing in the bay. It was strange, but the picture before her was assuaging something deep inside. She felt at peace here, which was odd because she'd never really felt such a sense of peace anywhere else.

So, she'd better not get too comfortable around here, she decided, calling to Sean and Danny to slow down ahead of her. She should just enjoy this little sojourn while she could.

By the time they had turned around and headed back, it was lunchtime. "How about some hamburgers and chips for lunch?" she suggested.

The boys didn't need to be asked twice as they headed for Sally's Place. The fresh air had made them all famished. Eden had to admit it was the first time she'd felt really hungry in a long time, and she enjoyed every mouthful of her food, including one of those fabulous milkshakes. At this rate it was just as well they were leaving tomorrow. She couldn't afford the extra kilos on her hips, even if she wasn't overweight.

Afterwards, they returned to the garage, and she breathed a double sigh of relief that Grant had gone out on a job. Now knowing he was a widower made her feel kind of awkward, not to mention she owed him an apology for calling him heartless over grounding his son. She wondered if Sean would tell his father that she was divorced.

"The part's on its way," Tom said, after Sean and Danny had excitedly relayed their morning's activities. "Should be here around four, but it's a big job. I'd say your car will probably be ready by lunch tomorrow."

"Thanks, Tom. That would be wonderful."

She forced herself to instill enthusiasm in her voice, but she really didn't feel as rushed now to be on her way to Brisbane. This sleepy little haven had snared her some, and that should worry her more than it did, she told herself. She couldn't let the lazy summer atmosphere get to her. There were plenty of other places she still had to see.

Tom mentioned a few touristy things they could do while they were here. Thanking him, she returned to the motel, where Danny promptly fell asleep watching television.

She took the opportunity to call her aunt in Sydney, not mentioning the car breaking down, and told her everything was fine. She tried calling her mother in Western Australia, but she didn't answer her mobile phone, so Eden left a message that everything was going well. Her mother would worry regardless.

Later in the afternoon, she and Danny went for another walk down to the beach where people were flying kites. She paid to let him fly one and they both had a wonderful time. She thought about dropping by the garage to see if the part had arrived — and Danny kept asking to see Sean — but that would mean her seeing Grant again.

No, she didn't want to do that. So, she gave it a wide berth and trusted that the car would be ready by lunchtime tomorrow.

She hoped.

Chapter Four

Grant didn't know whether to groan or not when he saw Eden Beresford and her son entering the half-filled restaurant.

"Oh look, there's Eden and Danny," Tom Ridgeway said, clearly not having the same reaction.

Sean jumped to his feet and waved across the restaurant. "Hey, Danny!"

The pair's heads snapped towards them. It was only fleeting, but Grant couldn't miss the quick dismay that feathered across Eden's face. Good. Sean had mentioned earlier that the woman was a divorcee, and while she didn't look the least like she was on the prowl, he didn't need his hormones kicking into gear where she was concerned. There was a definite sexual attraction between them, but at least she appeared as reluctant as he was to acknowledge it.

And then he watched her walk towards their table, and his body instantly reacted to firm breasts bouncing slightly beneath a creamy knit top, and to the soft sway of hips beneath the short pink skirt. She wasn't wearing stockings but her tanned, slim legs didn't need them. She reminded him of a delectable dessert... and very, very appetising.

She pasted on a smile as she came up to the

table. "Good evening," she murmured, her green eyes touching on him, then sliding away like the softest palm frond brushing his skin. He tried not to react.

Danny and Sean high-fived.

"Eden, I see you got my message," Tom said warmly.

"Yes, I did, Tom. Thanks very much."

"Message?" Grant said sharply, suddenly suspicious. His father had a certain light in his eyes ever since learning the woman was unattached, but Grant didn't want him getting any ideas. *He* wasn't interested. And the woman was only going to be in town for not more than a moment anyway.

Her smile slipped and her eyes darted from one to the other, clearly sensing an undercurrent now. "Er... yes. Tom sent a message to the hotel recommending this place for dinner," she said, explaining her presence here.

"Oh, he did, did he?" He shot his father a wry look and received what he considered a poker face in return. Is that why his father had suggested a night off from cooking? Dad's treat, he'd said.

Tom leaned back in his chair, looking very pleased with himself now. "That's right, I did send a message. I forgot to mention it earlier today, and I knew you wouldn't want to miss out while you're here, Eden. Charlie would never forgive me if I hadn't recommended his restaurant. He's got the best seafood restaurant in town."

Grant couldn't help the twist to his lips. "Charlie has the *only* seafood restaurant in town," he said, but he was just as cynical about his father. As soon as Sean had mentioned the woman's divorce, Tom Ridgeway must have got on the phone and instigated this meeting.

She stood there, her thin eyebrows pencilled together, as if trying to figure out how she'd come to be in the middle of something.

Tom indicated their table. "Why don't you and Danny join us?"

Grant could easily have kicked him.

She began to look even more uncomfortable. "No, that's fine, Tom. We don't want to intrude."

"Aw, Mum," Danny muttered.

"You're not intruding," Tom assured her, just as the owner of the restaurant came up to the table. "Charlie, do you mind if we put two tables together?"

Charlie beamed at them all. "Of course not."

Soon they were all playing musical chairs before Danny and Sean were happily seated next to each other. Eden sat next to his father and opposite *him*. With his back to the wall – literarily — Grant couldn't help but look at her.

She gave him a small smile then looked away, but that didn't seem to matter. Without warning, the smile slammed into him with the heated rush of his pulse as his body throbbed to life.

"Comfortable?"

For a split second, he thought someone was speaking to him, then realised his father was actually talking to Eden. Just as well. His body definitely wasn't comfortable right now.

Eden smiled. "Yes, thank you, Tom." She paused. "So, is there any special reason you're eating here tonight too?" she asked, a curious light in her green eyes making him wonder if she'd figured it out yet. It wouldn't be too hard.

"Not really," his father said. "I just like treating my son and grandson to something fancy once in a while."

Grant knew his father was playing matchmaker. Didn't he realise it was a waste of everyone's time? "I'm surprised you didn't invite the rest of the family as well, Dad," he drawled.

Tom didn't look the least bit discomforted. "Ryan and Jared were busy tonight. And Carly had some work to do at the gift shop."

Grant was both bemused and frustrated with his father. He doubted that Ryan and Jared would have been invited to dinner in the first place. And Carly had been doing a stocktake tonight, having told him in private she suspected one of her assistants was stealing from her. He'd drop by the store after dinner and see how she was going.

No, for some reason, his father had set his sights on Eden being perfect for his eldest son.

Him.

Eden's eyebrow rose. "Are they your

children, Tom?"

Tom chuckled. "Yes, but they're no longer children, I'm afraid. Except for Zoe. She's my three-year-old granddaughter."

"And the apple of her grandfather's eye, by the sounds of things," Eden teased.

"Naturally."

Just then Amy, their waitress, appeared and they spent the next few minutes deciding what to order. After that, a middle-aged couple dropped by their table and chatted for a few minutes. They'd been such good friends of his parents. Grant watched his father put on a brave face. His parents had been very happy for forty years until his mother's death a couple of years ago, but it must hurt his dad to see this other couple and not think of his beloved Sylvie. God, *he* still missed his mother. She'd been a wonderful woman, so loving and her family meaning everything to her. His parents' marriage had been perfect in his eyes.

Of course, he understood why his father wanted him to be happy, but it didn't mean he was looking to get married again and put down roots here. He planned on going back to Melbourne when the time was right, once the memory of Eve's death had dimmed for Sean. It had been so hard on his son losing his mother out of the blue like that. Dammit, in spite of their divorce *he* was having trouble coming to grips with the suddenness of her death himself.

So, he wasn't planning on getting involved anytime soon and certainly not with a woman who was in town for a mere five minutes. Hell, what was his father thinking anyway? It wasn't like either Eden or himself didn't have their own sons to think about. They weren't about to embark on a passionate, overnight affair. And it *would* be passionate on both their parts. He had no doubt about that.

Okay, so it *had* been a while since he'd had sex. He'd been faithful to his wife, even though they'd separated months before her death. But after leaving Melbourne and bringing Sean home to Opal Bay six months ago, he hadn't had much time to be with a woman. Sure, there'd been women interested in him, and one woman in particular whom he'd spent a weekend with in Port Macquarie, but his son had always been his priority. And while that woman had only been visiting from Sydney and had let him know she was ready to start up a long distance affair, he just hadn't been interested.

"Has the part arrived yet?" Eden asked, drawing him from his thoughts.

He went to speak but had to clear his throat

first. He didn't want her to hear any huskiness in his voice. "Yes. Come by at lunch tomorrow and the car should be ready." He'd try not to be there, but still, he felt a small twinge at not seeing her again.

"That's great," she said, but her voice gave nothing away. Yet her eyes did, and did he just catch a glimpse of disappointment at the back of them? Was it because she would be leaving but didn't want to go? And why did that send another rush of adrenaline through him?

"Eden, tell us," Tom began, "what are you doing in this neck of the woods anyway? Just passing through, or are you planning on holidaying along the coast somewhere?"

She took a sip of her water before answering, and Grant had the suspicion she was giving herself time to frame her words. "We've just spent three months in Sydney with relatives, and now we're on our way to Brisbane for another three months before we head back to Perth after Easter. So, I thought it would be a good idea to drive up the coast and see more of Australia."

"The two of you came for an extended holiday then?"

"Sort of." Grant saw her dart him a look beneath her lashes, as if to ask if all his family were into grilling a person. He hadn't discussed her with his father at all, but his ears had perked up when Sean had told them what he'd learned about her and Danny.

"Mum's divorced now," Danny said, joining in the conversation.

Eden rolled her eyes. "Thank you, Danny," she said wryly, briefly smiling at her son. She looked back at Tom and her smile faded. "My divorce came through a few months ago, so I decided to bring Danny to the east coast for a long holiday."

"See, I told you, Granddad," Sean piped up.

"Forgive my grandson," Tom said with a fond smile as he looked at Sean, then gave Eden a more sympathetic look. "Good for you, love."

She looked surprised, then murmured, "Thank you," and Grant watched her with a stab of sympathy. He knew how hard it was to start again.

"So, you have relatives over here?" his father asked.

She nodded. "My aunt and uncle live in Sydney. Actually, it's my mother's sister. They run... er... a family business in Sydney with an office in Brisbane. I've been helping out a little here and there. I'll do the same in Brisbane."

"What sort of business?" Grant asked, curious now.

She blinked as her eyes slid across to him.

"Temporary hire. Personnel that is, not machinery."

"That sounds like it would be a thriving business," Tom said.

"Yes, it is," she said, then looked relieved when Amy brought over some plates of food.

Grant knew she was skimming over information about herself and her family, and who could blame her? He recognised a fellow sufferer who'd needed to get away. It seemed to be that final step before picking up the pieces and putting a life back together.

The meals arrived then, and all-in-all it was a pleasant evening. Eden was personable and appeared to relax a little over a glass of wine. He was feeling a little more relaxed himself and could even appreciate her company for this one short-lived evening.

"Dad," Sean said, interrupting his thoughts.

"Can we go play pinball at Sally's now?"

Grant looked at his son and remembered how Sean had almost given him a heart attack by taking that boat out in the bay without adult supervision. "Have you forgotten you're grounded?"

"But you said I could show Danny around the place." Sean seemed to be pretending he didn't understand what was going on. They both knew that was a one-off thing.

Grant ignored that as he put his napkin down on the table. "It's time we went home." He caught Amy's attention as she went to pass their table.

"But Dad..." Sean began.

Grant gave him a meaningful look. "Don't push it, son." He returned his gaze to the teenage waitress. "The bill, thanks, Amy."

"Sure thing, Grant."

Eden picked up her purse. "We must go too.

We have a lot of driving to do tomorrow afternoon." She looked at Amy. "Can I have my bill too, please?"

The waitress frowned. "Oh, but aren't you all together?" she asked, looking from one to the other.

"No, I —"

"*I'm* paying the bill, Amy," Tom intervened. "All of it."

"Tom, no!" Eden scolded. "I can't let you do that."

He held up his hand to prevent further comment. "I asked you to sit at our table and I insist on paying."

"But —"

"It's no use arguing, Eden," Grant said, with some amusement, not the least bit surprised his father had insisted on paying. Tom Ridgeway was an old-fashioned guy. "It's easier to give in."

Tom chuckled. "See, listen to my son."

For a moment she looked like she would argue further, then she eased into a gracious smile. "Well, thank you, Tom. That's very nice of you."

After Tom paid the bill they all filed outside. Grant wouldn't have been male if he hadn't taken a quick look at Eden's long legs as she preceded him. She may not be showing as much leg as he'd seen in those shorts she'd worn yesterday back on the roadside, but she was one sexy lady!

He swallowed hard as he realised what he was doing. Bloody hell, what was the matter with him? He'd been mentally holding her at bay since meeting her, but now that he knew she wasn't attached to anyone, he couldn't seem to stop his body from overreacting to her. Dammit, what did it matter this once anyway? He wasn't going to see her again.

Out on the footpath, his father said, "Grant, would you and Sean walk Eden and Danny back to the motel? I need to go see someone."

The boys cheered.

Grant could have wrung his father's neck. It was best to leave things now. Tomorrow he'd be out when she collected her car and that would be that.

Eden looked dismayed. "No, that's okay. We don't need anyone to walk us back to the motel."

The boys groaned.

Tom ignored that. "Son, I have to go see Phil about some tyres. You can come along if you like..." He paused knowingly. "But I thought you'd much prefer to walk with Eden and Danny."

Grant swore to himself. The crafty old devil. His father knew very well he'd do almost anything rather than meet up with Phil. Anything but walk with Eden? This was just a ploy to get them together. Why couldn't his father just let it be?

He sighed and checked his watch. "Okay, Dad, but Sean and I will meet you back here in half an hour. If you're not here I'm going home."

Tom's smile was smooth and self-satisfied. "I'll be here."

Grant shot him a look that said he'd better be.

Eden thanked Tom again for the meal and said goodbye, before falling into step beside Grant. The boys scampered ahead, weaving in and out of small groups of people strolling along the footpath in the fading sunset. She liked the older man but wished he hadn't been so obvious about throwing her and his son together tonight. It was embarrassing and made her uncomfortable and no doubt Grant was too. His purposeful strides beside her were clear indication that he couldn't wait to get rid of her.

"You don't like this Phil then?" she asked, as she hurried to keep up.

He must have realised he'd been going too fast. His steps slowed to a more sedate pace. "It's not that. The man rarely takes a breath, that's all. He could talk underwater." He paused with a small smile. "There's a couple of other people around here like that as well."

His humour took her by surprise. And she wondered... "So, do you like it here? Apart from people who talk too much?" she teased.

His eyes said he appreciated her comment. "Sure I do. It's a great place."

"Have you lived here long?" she asked, suddenly wanting to know more about him.

He looked away. "Just over a year."

"Is that all?"

"I grew up here." His eyes stayed directly ahead. "Then I went to live in Melbourne."

She let that sink in. Funny how she thought of him more as a rugged type of guy than a city man. Perhaps it was the air he had about him. An element of being untamed even when he looked thoroughly civilised.

"Are you planning on settling down in Opal Bay for good now?"

He glanced at her then. "Is this payback for the interrogation my father gave you?"

She laughed. "No, but now that you've mentioned it..."

Another smile flashed then went so fast she thought she might have imagined it.

"Actually I'm not sure how long we'll be here. It all depends on Sean and when he's ready to go back to the city."

"Because of your wife's death?" She saw him stiffen. "Sorry, I shouldn't intrude like that."

He raised an eyebrow. "So you know I'm a widower?"

"I heard Sean mention it to Danny."

He gave a shake of his head. "Kids don't have a problem sharing anything with the world, do they?"

"No. Of course, when you want them to open up, they won't."

He looked at her in a moment of bonding. "Too true."

She decided she liked this connection between them. She wanted it to continue. For these few minutes anyway. "And they think they know everything as well. Have you noticed that?"

His mouth relaxed with sudden humour that

made her heartbeat kick. "Oh, I've noticed. I believe it gets worse as they get older."

"Will I slit my throat now or later?" she joked, and he gave a soft chuckle that coasted down her spine.

She caught her breath.

Their eyes held.

She was the one to break eye contact and look directly ahead. "Sean said he was grounded because he took a rowing boat out in the bay."

"That's right," he said, and she glanced at him again, seeing his mouth had tightened and the hint of awareness between them disappearing with the serious of the subject. "The bay looks calm, but it's easy enough to drown. He knows better."

"Good decision." She hesitated, then said, "I apologise for thinking you were heartless over grounding him."

He flicked her a surprised glance. "Thanks."

"I just wanted to say that before I leave."

He nodded.

They walked in silence for a bit, then he called out to the boys ahead to slow down and to check for cars before crossing the road. After they had safely crossed, they raced over to the well-lit children's play area that was part of the motel.

"So when you go back to Melbourne you'll be looking for a new job I suppose?" she said.

"No, I already have a job waiting for me. I'm a mechanical engineer and my old boss said he'd have me back whenever I'm ready."

Her eyes widened. "So you're not a mechanic then?"

He gave a short laugh. "Don't worry. I was a mechanic before I became an engineer. I know what I'm doing with your car."

"That's a relief," she joked.

"My father wouldn't have me working with him if I didn't have the qualifications. He's a stickler for things like that. And rightly so."

She nodded in agreement. "Your father's a really nice man. I didn't expect him to pay for our dinner."

"Dad's generous like that." He darted her a sideways glance. "But he's usually not so manipulative."

She was startled that he brought it up. She'd known what Tom had been doing, but knowing that Grant knew too, had embarrassed her.

She gave a small shrug. "That's okay. He's just got it wrong, that's all."

There was almost a hush at her words...

Like everything there on the main street had faded away...

Even the sound of their footsteps...

She was only aware of them coming to a standstill, of him facing her, the look in his blue eyes suddenly very much a male. "How wrong?" he murmured.

Her throat went dry. "Er... totally wrong. I mean... it won't do any good throwing us together like this anyway, will it?" She licked her lips and tried to hold onto her composure but suspected she was losing it. "I'm leaving tomorrow, and we'd have to act fast if we were going to do anything, right?" She knew she was babbling too much but couldn't seem to stop herself.

His eyes narrowed. "Is that an invitation for tonight?"

"God no!"

He gave a startled laugh. "Thanks very much."

She pulled a face. "Sorry, but you know what I

mean."

"Yeah, I do actually." A hint of regret in his eyes echoed inside her. "Any other time but now."

Her heart leapt. "Maybe," she managed to say, amazed she could admit even that. She wasn't used to being wanted by a man other than Martin, and even then... "I'm really not looking to get involved, Grant. Not even for a night."

He held her gaze, then slowly nodded. "At least we can agree on that. I'm not looking for anything either. Not a night. Certainly not more than that."

She let out a slow breath. What if his answer had been different? What if... And how the heck had they come to this point in a mere conversation?

All at once, the main street came back into focus. Sounds came alive again. The light breeze from the bay whisked a piece of paper in the air. The world continued. It had only been a moment in time between them. A moment now gone.

Just then, someone called out Grant's name.

Eden turned and saw a young, dark-haired woman waving at them from one of the stores on the other side of the road. The woman was just locking the door of "Gifts & Things", but she obviously wanted to speak to Grant.

"That's my sister," Grant said, as they waited for her to cross the road. Eden couldn't help but take a more interested look now.

The woman reached them. "Thanks for waiting, guys." She held out her hand to Eden and smiled, looking very attractive. "Hi. I'm Carly, Grant's sister. I saw you and your son walking today with Sean."

Eden shook her hand, figuring that Carly was around her own age. "I'm Eden Beresford." She indicated the boys playing on the swings in the motel playground. "And that's my son, Danny."

"I know." She laughed. "Nothing's a secret in this place, Eden."

"I'm starting to see that." Though why she and Danny should be of interest to anyone was beyond her. They had slipped into town in a tow truck, and they'd slip out again as easily.

"Sean tells me your car broke down outside town."

"Yes, but I'm leaving tomorrow. You have a lovely town here."

"I love it," Carly said enthusiastically, then tilted her head. "Pity you couldn't stay a bit longer."

Eden wanted to ask why, but she had the feeling she wouldn't like the answer. Perhaps the whole town liked to matchmake? Heck, even if she and Grant didn't hit it off, then there'd always be Carly's two other brothers, right?

As soon as she thought it, she grimaced inwardly. She was probably doing the woman an injustice. Carly was smiling at her in a friendly fashion, nothing more. She was just being nice.

The other woman spun towards Grant, an excited look in her eyes. "You'll never believe it. Debbie's decided to leave. She's going to live with her boyfriend in Sydney."

He frowned. "She's been threatening to do that for ages."

"Yes, I know but this time she's really gone and done it. She's already handed in her resignation. It's such a relief."

He looked pleased. "That's good news then. It's saved a lot of hassle for you."

Carly nodded, then bit her lip. "Except that now it's left me in a bit of a bind. I know a couple of people who might be interested, but I'm not sure they could cope with being rushed off their feet at times." She looked at Eden, seeming to realise she was talking out of turn and turned back to her brother. "Well, if you hear of anyone suitable wanting a part-time job, Grant, let me know, will you? They don't need any experience. As long as they've got common sense and are reliable, I'll be happy with that."

"Sure, sis, I'll keep an ear out."

Eden stood there listening to them and suddenly the wildest idea occurred to her. It had been building inside her ever since she'd come to this little bayside town. If ever there was a moment in life when a person just *knew* something meaningful was about to happen, it was now.

Right now.

Without a doubt, she knew she was at another crossroad in her life, much like she'd known to take the turn-off to Opal Bay yesterday when she suspected the car had been about to stop. And now, this once, she felt like she was in the right place at the right time.

So very right, she decided, her gaze darting across the road to Danny playing on the swings beside Sean. Her son had been really happy here the last twenty-four hours.

She couldn't turn back to Carly quick enough. "What would the hours be?" she blurted out before she could stop herself, and saw Grant look at her strangely.

Carly blinked too. "Er... ten until three Monday to Thursday. I'm here on a Friday and weekends, but I also have another lady helping out then too. Why? Do you have someone in mind?"

"I'd love to apply for the job."

"What!" Grant said.

Carly's eyes widened in startled surprise as well. "I'd love to have you but..." She darted an uncertain look at brother. "I'm not sure how we would work this. You're only here for a short time, aren't you?"

Eden knew she couldn't let this opportunity pass without a fight. She had to get the job. She just had to. She could see it was exactly what she and Danny both needed.

"Carly, let me explain. I've been helping my aunt and uncle in Sydney in the family business. And now I'm on my way north to work for their Brisbane office for three months." She took a breath. "But I'm not really needed there. They were only being kind in giving me work to do."

The other woman's forehead had creased, as if taking all this on board. "I see."

Eden didn't want to beg but she would if

necessary. "You said yourself that I should stay here longer. I agree. It *would* be a pity if I left." She thought of something else. "And it'll give you time to find someone more suitable too."

"Yes, that's true."

A ray of hope raced through Eden. "And if you don't think I've got what it takes, then I'll leave without question." She gave a weak smile. "Anyway, I have to go back to Perth eventually, so you know I won't be hanging around forever, right?" She heard the boys' laughter float across the road. This was so important to her now.

To her and Danny.

"I'd really love to stay in Opal Bay for a while. My son's happy here and I'm sure I would be too. It's exactly what we need." She cleared her throat. "It feels so right, you know."

Carly studied her for a long moment, then

she glanced at Grant, seeming to be coming to a decision. "Dad *was* quite impressed with her," she said, as if bouncing her thoughts off her brother. Grant started to say something, but Carly waved that aside. She broke into a smile. "And that's good enough for me."

Eden's breath stopped. "Oh my gosh! I've got the job?" she said, vaguely aware of Grant's sharp intake of breath but not caring right then.

Carly nodded. "If you want it." She paused. "But tell you what. You think on it and come see me here at the shop tomorrow morning at ten. If you're still interested, the job's yours."

Eden started to breathe again. "Thank you! Oh God, thank you so much!"

"You're very welcome, Eden."

She couldn't believe it. She could actually stay here in this wonderful town for another three months. She wasn't one to do things on the spur of the moment. Hell, it had taken her six months after the split with Martin before she'd even thought about coming to the east coast for an extended period. But this time she knew she had to jump at this chance to stay... to heal...

"Sorry to put a damper on this," Grant said, drawing her attention back to him. "But don't you both think you've forgotten something important?"

Eden's heart wobbled. "Wh..what?"

"Where are you going to live? It's summer holidays. Everything's at a high premium right now. Whatever was available to rent has already been taken."

Eden's heart dropped to her feet. "Oh no! I didn't think of that." The disappointment was immense. How could she let herself get so carried away about this without thinking it through first?

There were so many considerations. What was the matter with her?

"Eden," Carly said slowly, as if she were thinking hard, "I don't know your money situation but if you could afford it you could stay at the motel. There might be some vacancies. Jake may have had a cancellation and I bet he would even give you a reduced rate if you're staying so long."

Eden's enthusiasm began to return. This was a once in a lifetime opportunity. "That's a very real option." Then she bubbled over and smiled. "Yes, I can do that." Right now she'd even pitch a tent on the beach.

"Great!" Carly said excitedly. Then she glanced at her watch. "Listen, I have to go collect Zoe from Maggie's place. That's my three-year-old daughter," she told Eden. "You think about it all and let me know tomorrow." She looked at her brother. "See you at home later, Grant." She dashed back across the road to a car parked under a street light outside her store.

Eden stood there watching her, amazed at how life could change in a split second. Carly didn't know it but she was an angel in disguise.

"Are you sure this is what you want to do?"

She looked up at Grant and gave a shaky laugh. "I think I just might be a little loco, don't you?"

"Yes." He wasn't amused.

She sobered. "This is something I want to do. *Need* to do, actually. I didn't realise it but after the divorce —" She saw his eyes narrow. She cut herself off, not wanting to go on about it. They both knew what it was like to need a fresh start.

Sean called out to his father right then and the moment was broken. She and Grant started across the road towards the boys still playing on the swings.

As they reached the other side, another problem occurred to her and her step faltered as she reached the curb. "Oh no, I haven't got anyone to look after Danny while I'm working. And I can't leave him sitting in the motel all day." She would only be working five hours but it was too long to leave him alone. There was suddenly so much that needed to be considered. It seemed overwhelming all at once.

"You could always get a babysitter," Grant suggested, an odd kindness in his voice as they reached the entrance to the motel playground.

She stopped walking, her heart lifting. "Yes, I could, couldn't I? It would have to be someone responsible though. I won't leave my son with just anyone."

He stopped walking too. "Most people

around here are responsible. Jake would probably know someone who could help. Ask him when you ask about the room."

Things were starting to fall into place. "I'll do that."

"You *do* realise that summer holidays finish at the end of January? What about Danny's schooling?"

She'd already thought that through before coming to the east coast. "It didn't seem worth it to enroll him in school in Sydney, so I've been doing home schooling. But I guess I could enroll him in school here for a couple of months. He'd think that was great, especially if Sean's there."

There was a moment's silence.

He lifted a brow. "So, you're really determined to do this?" he said, an odd look in his eyes.

"Yes, I'm really going to do this."

He stuck his hands in his pockets and turned away, almost jerkily. "Sean! It's time to go home now."

"Aah, Dad," came the instant grumble.

"Now." There was no disputing the authority in Grant's voice.

The boys started to get off the swings... slowly... reluctantly...

Something occurred to Eden. She reached out and put her hand on Grant's arm. "Don't say anything to Danny, will you?"

He tensed and glanced down to where they touched. She felt a tingle in her palm as he looked up again, and she saw something deep lurking in his eyes. "So, you're really *not* sure about this?" His voice sounded thick and there seemed to be more than words between them. In fact, there seemed to be something happening on a whole different level.

She quickly dropped her hand, ignoring the thumping of her heart. "No. I'm sure." *Sure I don't want to get involved with you.* She forced herself to concentrate. This was about Danny, not Grant. "But I want to speak to him first. He's been through a lot."

Grant nodded just as the boys reached them and before too long it was time to say good night. Then she and Danny walked into the motel as Grant and his son walked away in the other direction. Danny chatted non-stop and her heart swelled with love, and more than ever she believed this was the right thing to do. Despite all the problems she still had to sort out, for the first time in a long time, she felt happy.

And it was odd, but she felt good about seeing more of the Ridgeways too, though she tried not to think about seeing Grant Ridgeway again. She wasn't sure why, but there was a connection to him and his family that seemed very real.

Then she wrinkled her nose at herself, unable to discount the obvious. Apart from Jake here at the motel, the Ridgeways were the *only* people she knew in town.

Chapter Five

She just hoped Carly didn't have second thoughts overnight. She wasn't going to tell her mother yet, nor her aunt and uncle. Not until it was all settled.

Yet in all honesty she couldn't take the job unless Danny approved. As much as she thought he would like to stay here, she needed to ask him and know for certain before she burned her bridges, though she hated the thought of disappointing him if it all fell through. He'd had too many disappointments in his short life, so she'd have to be careful how she phrased things.

"Danny, you like it here in Opal Bay, don't you?" she said, keeping her tone casual.

His eyes stayed glued to the television. "Yeah, it's great."

She waited a few seconds. "It would be nice to live here for a while, don't you think?"

He jack-knifed off the pillows. "Are we going to stay here, Mum?"

"It's just a thought. For a couple of months anyway. I'd rather stay here than go to Brisbane, wouldn't you?"

His eyes lit up. "Oh wow! That would be so cool! I'd be able to be best friends with Sean and everything. He knows some great stuff. He's even got a go-kart."

"Really?" She was glad he was enthusiastic, but she was feeling a little uneasy too. God, she hoped she wasn't getting his hopes too high. "Look, honey, I'm just thinking about it, okay? Don't get too excited yet. There's a lot to consider first."

He flopped back down against the pillows and sighed. "Okay, Mum. I understand."

Her heart constricted and she prayed that it all worked out. Her son deserved to be happy.

And then she realised something. She didn't have to answer to anyone, so whether the job eventuated or not, why couldn't she simply stay here in Opal Bay anyway? She had the money and the time, and she really didn't need to go to Brisbane. She and Danny could stay here in this idyllic little place hidden from the world and enjoy their visit. Her aunt and uncle — more importantly

— her mother would just have to understand.

The bell over the door tinkled as Eden entered "Gifts & Things" at ten the next morning. She'd left Danny back in the motel room under threat of not letting anyone into the room and as soon as this was sorted she'd hurry back. The shop was practically across the road from the motel anyway.

"Hello there," Carly greeted with a bright smile, seeming to be the only person in the place. "So, you're still interested in the job then?"

"Absolutely." She held her breath as she walked towards the counter. "It *is* still available, isn't it?"

"If you want it."

Relief launched through Eden's veins. "Oh

yes!”

Carly looked pleased as well. “That’s wonderful. Do you think you can start next Monday? I can hold the fort until then.”

“Perfect.” It was only Wednesday and that would give her time to get everything sorted out. “Thank you so much, Carly. I really mean that.”

“Hey, you’ll be helping me too. And it’ll be so nice to have someone my own age working with me for a change. Debbie was a little young, and Nancy who helps out sometimes is in her fifties. A lovely lady, but we don’t have a lot in common.”

Eden didn’t say it, but she wondered if she had a lot in common with Carly herself. *She* wasn’t a party girl, and she had no idea whether Carly was, though owning this store was a big responsibility for Carly no doubt.

“By the way.” Carly’s voice drew Eden from

her thoughts. "I was thinking of your living situation and realised the house next door to us is available. Well, it's a cottage really. Pete Wylie stopped by just before and he was saying that the person who'd booked had to leave due to a family emergency. Pete was going to start advertising but if you wait, I'll give him a call and see what's doing. He might lease it out to you for a couple of months. It's fully-furnished."

Eden dare not breathe. "That would be wonderful," she murmured, but she was wondering about the "us". It had to mean Grant and Sean would be her next-door neighbour too. Good for Danny. Not so good for *her*.

Still, she held her breath while Carly called. The conversation went well and when she hung up, she said, "Pete's happy to lease it out to you, but it would have to be a minimum six month's contract.

That covers him in case you wanted to leave early. He'd have to find lodgers for the rest of the year, if that were the case. It's quieter but people like to come here then, but he could still lose money if it was vacant for even a week."

Eden understood. "That would be fine." More than fine. Six months in this place sounded like heaven.

Then something caught at her and she realised she owed it to Carly to be fair. "Are you happy with that too, Carly? I'm not sure what I'll be doing after six months," she pointed out. "If I can't stay longer, I could be leaving you in the lurch."

Carly's face softened. "Thank you, Eden. I appreciate your concern but if things work out, I'm quite happy to have you here for six months. Longer even. It's up to you."

Eden felt like she was being cosseted in a warm

cocoon. It made her want to cry with happiness.

She cleared her throat. "I keep saying thank you, but I do really mean it."

"I know."

"Well, I'd better go and tell Danny." She turned towards the door.

"You can bring him to the store, if you like." Carly's words had her spinning back to face the other woman. "He can sit in the back room and watch television, just until school starts. The only thing I ask is that he's not to be running around the store and that if he breaks anything you pay for it."

The offer stole Eden's breath. She had to swallow hard and blink back tears before she could speak. "That's such a generous offer," she whispered. "Thank you."

"I know how hard it is being a single mum. I'm one myself."

Eden hid her surprise. Sean had mentioned a Zoe to Danny, so Eden had assumed Carly's father lived with them, though she hadn't really thought about it. "Again, thank you so much."

Carly smiled with pleasure. "You'd better go get yourself organised, neighbour."

Eden's steps were light as she went back to the motel and told her son the good news.

He hugged her. "Oh wow, Mum! We're gonna stay?" He hugged her again. "Oh wow!"

She laughed and spun him around the room, then gave him a big hug back. "And we have a house to stay in too."

"Oh Mummy, really?"

Her heart melted. He only ever called her Mummy when something affected him deeply. "Yes, honey. Really."

"Can we go tell Sean right now?"

"Why not? I have to see if our car's ready anyway."

Ten minutes later they walked into the garage workshop. Grant had his head under the bonnet of another car, but he straightened up as she and Danny approached.

"No need to ask if things went well," he said, his glance over her face making her heart pick up speed. Then he darted a look at Danny and smiled. "I can see you've told him."

"How can you tell?" she joked, and their eyes caught.

"Is Sean here, Mr. Ridgeway?" Danny said, looking around eagerly.

Grant broke eye contact with her. "He went to talk to Bill at the barber shop next door."

Danny looked up at her. "Mum, can I go find him?"

She nodded, seeing the shop from where she was standing. "Sure, honey, but that's as far as you go. Nowhere else, okay?"

"Okay." He raced off.

Tom came out of the office. "You're staying then?"

"Yes. And it's all due to you, Tom, thank you. Your daughter trusts your judgment."

"She's a good girl," he mused. "And I'm happy you're staying. We need some young people around here permanently. And I believe we're going to be neighbours as well."

"Neighbours?" Grant said sharply.

It wasn't hard to sense that Grant wasn't happy about all this. Still, she tried to remain positive. "Yes, Carly's killing me with kindness. She's arranged a furnished house for six months through someone called Pete Wylie. Apparently, the people who were supposed to lease it pulled out at the last minute."

Tom looked at his son. "It's Bayside Cottage. Right next door to us."

Grant's eyes shuttered. "I see."

Tom beamed at Eden. "I think it's great."

She had too, but now she was thinking that taking that particular house wasn't such a good idea. "Of course, I haven't signed the lease yet. I can try and get somewhere else. I don't want to be in everyone's face."

"Don't be ridiculous," Tom said, dismissing her concern. "We'd love to have you and Danny as neighbours."

She wasn't sure about that. Certainly not about Grant.

"Now," Tom said. "You're car's ready, Eden. I took it for a test drive before." He glanced at his son. "Grant, how about you go with Eden up to Bayside Cottage. The kids can go as well. I'll mind the   shop."

Grant's mouth flattened in a grim line. "It's probably best Eden goes by herself."

"Yes, that's fine," Eden hurriedly intervened. "I have to go get the keys from this Pete first anyway."

"Do you know where he lives?" Tom asked.

"No, but I have the address. Just point me in the right direction."

"It's easier if Grant goes with you."

Just then, the phone rang, and Tom left them to it, but not before he winked at Eden as he passed by. She blinked. Was the wink telling her not to worry about Grant's attitude, or just a friendly wink to say he was happy with her working for his daughter and becoming his neighbour? She suspected it was both.

The sound of Grant closing the bonnet of the car echoed loudly in the garage and made her jump. It wasn't an angry slam, but she knew he wasn't pleased by the turn of events.

Great. A hostile neighbour before she'd even moved in.

"Look, I'm sorry if this has made you uncomfortable," she said, but she was beginning to get her back up. She wasn't staying in Opal Bay because of him, and she couldn't help it if his family were so friendly. She wasn't trying to come onto him either.

He shrugged and turned away. "It doesn't affect me whether you live next door or not."

Yeah, right.

"I promise you won't know we're there." And it was a promise she intended to keep.

He sent her an ironic look. "I'm sure Danny

will let me know he's there."

She stiffened. Not liking *her* was one thing. Not liking her *son* was another.

She raised her chin. "Don't worry. I'll keep my son well away if that's the problem."

Irritation crossed his face. "Don't be so prickly. I didn't mean that at all."

Her eyes widened. "Me? I'm not the one —"

He turned away as the boys came strolling into the garage. "Hey, you two," he cut across her. "Want to go for a ride."

Both boys were there in a flash. "Sure."

Grant jerked his head at her car. "Hop in the back seat."

She held out her hand. "The keys please. I'll drive."

"No, you'd better let me. I want to make sure it's working all right."

"But Tom said —"

"It's fine, I know. But I'm still driving. Just as a precaution."

"Did anyone ever tell you that you're —"

"Charming?"

"Obstinate."

"No. Never."

"Really? I find that hard to believe."

Out of nowhere, his eyes turned sensual. "Do you now?" he murmured, his hard mouth relaxing, those blue eyes snagging hers until she almost expected he would pull her up against him. For a split second she leaned just that little bit towards him.

"Dad, are we going yet?"

She froze.

So did Grant, then his face closed up and he rotated on his heels and headed for her car. She heard him talking to Sean.

And she noted he still had her keys.

Fifteen minutes later — with Grant driving — they were pulling into a long driveway around the other side of the bay, after stopping off at Pete Wylie's place to get the house keys first. He seemed a nice man.

"See, that's my house over there," Sean was telling Danny from the back seat, pointing to the house on the next block.

"Cool!"

Then Eden saw the house ahead. *Her* house. Temporary but still hers for now. "Oh my God," she whispered.

Grant shot her a sideways look. "What's the matter?"

"It's a real cottage."

"Yeah, so?"

"It's beautiful."

"Is that all? I thought there was a problem."

She shook her head. How did she say to him that this was exactly what she'd dreamed of while growing up, rather than the large empty house she and her mother had shared. This one was on the small side, but it was a seaside cottage bearing the charm and character of yesteryear, where one could laze away on tranquil days. She could already see the log fire roaring on a winter's night, or the light breeze skipping through the open doors on a summer's day.

"Mummy, look at that," Danny said excitedly, as the car pulled up in the driveway. "Can we take it, Mum? Please say we can?"

As if she'd say no. She grinned at her son. "Just try and stop me," she teased, but she knew she was giving Grant fair warning. She wasn't about to give this house up now that she'd seen it.

She felt him looking at her, but she avoided his eyes.

Danny undid his seatbelt and leaned over the seat to kiss her on the cheek. "Thanks, Mum." Then he was opening his door. "Let's go inside and see my room, Sean. I bet it's fantastic."

She climbed out of the car in case Grant wanted to open a discussion about it. As far as she was concerned there was nothing to discuss now. Thankfully, the children's presence impeded any further talk as they went inside.

The house was everything she and Danny wanted and more. Danny's bedroom window even faced Sean's bedroom window, and she heard them planning to send each other signals using torches.

"Mum, this is so great," Danny said, doing a skip around the kitchen. Then he gave her a hug. He was hugging her a lot these last few days, and it pleased her.

"Yes, it is."

"Come on, Danny," Sean said. "Let me show you around outside."

They started to race off and she quickly followed them onto the verandah. "Danny, I want you to promise me you won't go near the bay."

"I won't, Mum. I promise."

She relaxed. "Okay."

Then the boys ran down the steps and around the house and she and Grant watched them. Tears pricked her eyes.

"Are you okay?"

She swiped her hand over them. "I've got something in my eye."

"Let me take a look."

She quickly swiped again. "No, it's fine now."

She blinked rapidly then pasted on a smile. "See."

He didn't look convinced but said nothing more. "So this place will do for you and Danny?"

"It's perfect."

He held her eyes, then gave a brief nod. "Good."

Surprise stole her breath for a moment. Then, "You don't have to be nice just because I said you weren't, you know."

His lips quirked. "I believe you called me obstinate."

All at once, light-heartedness filled her. "Oh yeah, I forgot."

He chuckled and she laughed back at him. Giggled, really.

Then his face turned serious. "Look, Eden, I know I've not been as... friendly as the others, but I'm glad you've found somewhere for you and your son to take a break. Sometimes that's what we need to help recover from the dirt life dishes out to us."

For the first time, she felt like her heartache was being shared. She sensed his pain too. "Thanks. I know you have your reasons and I'm fine with that. Seriously, I just want to make a new life for me and Danny. And if I'm to be a good Mum I need to get my self-respect back. This job and this house will help me do that."

"He hurt you a great deal, didn't he?"

She nodded. "Yes, he did." Then she took a shuddering breath. "But it's not the end of the world. I have my son." She forced a smile and gestured around her. "And now I have a place to live. And I have a job. What more can I ask?"

He scanned her face. Then the sound of the boys running back towards the house carried on the breeze and his expression relaxed into a smile. "So you're counting your blessings, are you? Lady, you have *no* idea what you're letting yourself in for with those next door neighbours over there." He indicated the Ridgeway house.

She was amazed at the pleasure that ran through her when he smiled at her like that. Warmth ran through her and for once she allowed it to continue. "Yes, I do. Carly and Tom are lovely," she teased, deliberately leaving him out of it.

"Let's see if you can say that about my two brothers."

Her brow lifted. "Oh?" Was there something she needed to know?

"I'm joking, Eden. Ryan and Jared are great guys. They have their own places, and you'll get to meet them eventually. There are various other relatives dotted around the place as well."

"Sounds like the Ridgeways are a big

family." She loved the thought of a large happy family.

"Big enough."

The boys reached the porch and excitedly babbled on about how fantastic this was all going to be, and she silently had to agree.

Then Grant held out the car keys towards her. "All yours now, milady. You can drive us back to Pete's to tell him the good news."

All at once she felt nervous driving with him in the car, but she soon pushed that feeling aside. She was in charge of her family and had been since Martin left. She wasn't about to go all soft and feminine just because a good-looking man like Grant was in the area.

Back at the garage, Tom came out to greet them. "How did it go? Do you like the house?"

"It's beautiful, Tom, and I can move in right

now. Isn't that wonderful?" She knew she was gushing but couldn't help herself.

"It certainly is, Eden."

Some imp inside her made her turn to Grant. "Do you think Sean can come with me and Danny for the afternoon? It will be fun for them to explore more of the house and backyard."

"Only if you allow me to bring lunch later," he quipped, then seemed to realise what he'd said.

Too late. The boys were already hooting with excitement. "That would be lovely," she said sweetly, even though her heart was thudding like she was in a race.

"Great!" Tom said, beaming. "Now, you're going to need help taking your luggage to the house." He darted a look at Grant and opened his mouth to speak again but she held up her hand.

"I can do it myself, thanks. I have my car

and that's all I need." Not giving him a chance to argue, she took out her purse. "Now, if you'll give me the bill I'll settle up."

Life was good and getting better by the minute.

Chapter Six

A few hours later, Grant could hear the boys playing as he came around the side of the cottage and saw Sean pushing Danny in the go-kart in the backyard. They were laughing. It warmed him to see his son so happy. It was nice to see Danny having a good time too.

They were too busy to notice him, so he let them be as he stepped up onto the verandah, then stopped dead when he saw Eden lying in the hammock. She was asleep and for some reason he couldn't stop himself from taking a moment to watch her. A light breeze caressed her face and the warm sun dappled over the wood decking around her and he just couldn't seem to look away. No doubt she was exhausted from recent events, he mused, then realised he was softening too much towards her.

Okay, so she was a nice lady. And she was a sexy lady too. Yet he'd seen nice, sexy ladies here before. Many a woman had made it clear they were up for a holiday affair. So why not Eden? What was different about her? His hand tightened on the paper bag he carried. It was best he didn't think about that.

He must have made a sound because her eyes opened and she blinked, then sat up. "Grant!" She ran her fingers through her hair. "Oh goodness, I wasn't supposed to fall asleep. I was just resting for a moment." All at once panic flared in her eyes and she quickly looked around. "Where's Danny?"

"Don't worry. He's with Sean. They're playing over there."

Her shoulders relaxed. "At least they didn't go off by themselves."

Grant felt his jaw tighten. "Sean wouldn't dare after last time."

She gave a sympathetic nod, then her gaze flickered down to the paper bag in his hand.

"Lunch, as promised," he said. "Fish and chips. Is that okay?"

"Of course. It's very thoughtful of you."

"I wanted to make sure Sean wasn't being too much trouble," he pointed out, making sure she knew it was about his son and not her.

A knowing light entered her eyes. "You could have just called me on my mobile."

Alright, so he wanted to make sure she was okay too. This was a big step for her staying here and everything entailed with her new, but temporary, life.

Thankfully, the boys came rushing up the steps then and whooped for joy when they heard what was for lunch. In next-to-no-time they were eating at the patio table but as soon as the boys were finished, they ran off again to play. Grant wasn't sure he should have enjoyed it all so much. It was all too... cosy for him. He didn't do cosy these days. Come to think of it, he wasn't sure he ever did.

"Can I ask you a personal question, Grant?" Eden asked, cutting through his thoughts.

He felt himself tense but said, "Shoot."

"I was just wondering. How did your wife

die?" She hesitated. "I only want to know for Sean's sake. I don't want to say or do anything to upset him about his mother."

Something shifted inside his chest. It moved him that she cared. "It was a car accident."

She inhaled sharply. "How tragic."

"Yes, it was. We were separated at the time, but I was still very much involved in Sean's life."

She paused, then, "He seems a well-adjusted kid, considering."

"Thank you."

"You've done a good job raising him."

He appreciated her comment. "Thanks. You're doing a good job with Danny too." He was only speaking the truth. He liked that she put her son first. She was a good mother, and he liked her as a person.

But not too much, he warned himself. She

may be a good mother and a good person, but she was also a very attractive woman. Too attractive for his peace of mind.

She smiled. "We have a lot in common."

Something kicked inside him, sending warning bells through his veins. "Yes, we do." He pushed to his feet to put an end to the conversation. "I must get back to the garage."

"Of course." She stood up too, and smiled almost shyly. "Thanks so much for lunch."

"My pleasure," he said before he could stop himself. And realised that was true. It had definitely been his pleasure.

He left then.

True or not, he'd leave it at that.

###

Eden spent the next few hours unpacking their clothes and making herself familiar with the house. Thankfully, it being a holiday rental and fully furnished, she didn't have to worry about anything else. There was plenty of fresh linen and cutlery and all the furniture was modern, clean and comfortable. Then at four o'clock she drove the boys the short distance to town to get some provisions from the small supermarket. It was close to the garage, so they popped in briefly but only Tom was there. Eden wasn't sure why she was disappointed that Grant had gone out on a job, and she mentally scolded herself as she drove back to the cottage. She was beginning to like seeing him too much.

Of course, it was probably because she couldn't get the thought of how his wife had died out of her head. He hadn't elaborated and she respected his privacy. It was interesting that he and his wife had been separated at the time though. She couldn't help but wonder why. Naturally, she was interested *only* because of her own separation before the divorce. As she'd said to Grant, they had a lot in common.

She was still wondering about it later that evening after Danny had gone to bed, but she pushed it aside. It was time to face the inevitable and phone her mother in Perth, then her aunt and uncle in Sydney. She could feel the beginnings of a headache coming on just thinking about it.

"Why the devil did you go and do that, Eden?" Regina Blake's exasperated tones came down the line. "You were supposed to be coming back home and now you're telling me you're thrashing about in some Godforsaken place on the East Coast and that I'll *maybe* see you sometime in the future?"

Eden sighed. "Mum, it's a little place called Opal Bay and it's not that far away from Sydney.

Only a couple of hours, tops," she said, deliberately minimising the time.

"I've never heard of it."

"Not many people have. And that's good. That's why it isn't too touristy. It's too small to compete with the other tourist places along the coast."

"Sounds a bit too boring for me."

"Lots of people would give up their credit cards to live in Opal Bay."

"Not me."

Eden could almost see her mother's shudder. She gave a choked laugh. "Mum, listen. They *do* know how to eat with a knife and fork around here."

"Why, Eden?" Her mother ignored her comment. "Why stay there and work in some little gift store when you can have such a good life here at home? Dammit, you and my grandson should be relaxing here in Perth and getting over your divorce."

"Mum, I was only staying at your place temporarily. Don't forget I wasn't staying for good."

"I know but I was so looking forward to having you here longer. And then I wanted to help set you up in your own place."

Eden's heart softened. "Yes, I know but I've realised I'm not ready to come home yet. Please understand. I *want* to do this. Please Mum, stop fussing."

"I'm not fussing," she scolded lightly, but they both knew she was. "It's just that I worry about you and Danny."

"We're doing fine. Danny's already made a friend." She could feel her breath catch just saying the words. "He's having fun again, Mum. This is a perfect place for a child to run free and enjoy himself."

There was a pause. "Good then," Regina said, resistance draining from her voice. "What about you, honey?"

"Any fitter and I'll be in the Guinness Book of Records."

Her mother didn't laugh. "I hate seeing you still suffer over that jerk. I never liked him, you know."

"I know, Mum."

"If only I could help more to take away your pain, honey."

"You can, Mum. Be happy for me and Danny."

"Six months you say?"

"Yes."

"And after that?"

"I'll come home."

"I might visit you sometime."

It sounded like a mild threat and Eden had to smile, even as she hoped her mother wouldn't visit. She needed this time to herself. She needed to keep stretching her wings without a mother hen watching over her. "You'll be very welcome, Mum."

Regina let out a slow breath. "I guess there's no use pushing you, Eden. You always did things in your own time."

"And who am I like?"

Her mother laughed, then they finished the call and Eden hung up with a lighter heart. That was one thing out of the way. Now she could get on with the next six months.

Eden had a good night's sleep and woke the next morning with a feeling of excitement. Firstly, she needed to wash some clothes and do bits and pieces around the place, then she'd take Danny for a long walk and become familiar with the local streets. It was great to know she didn't have to rush or worry too much about anything until she started work on Monday.

Surprisingly, no one from next door stopped by that day. She half-expected Grant would, considering he had been so thoughtful by bringing them fish and chips yesterday. No sight of Sean either. Danny had asked to go over to see him, but Eden said no. Sean was probably helping out at the garage, she pointed out, much to Danny's disappointment. Besides, she didn't want to intrude on their lives too much. They owed her nothing. They had their own lives to lead.

Mid-afternoon Danny was so restless she drove him to the playground in town near the motel, intending to take him for a walk on the sand after that, though she kept away from the garage at the other end of the main street. But Danny was like a sad little puppy as he swung aimlessly on the swing, missing his friend, and not interested in a couple of other children playing there with their parents.

Eden's heart cramped as she sat on the wooden bench. How quickly children attached themselves to others. For a moment she wondered if she'd done the right thing by staying here. Then she admonished herself. Of course she had. Danny had to accept there were times when he needed to depend on himself.

So, she put on a bright smile and called to Danny to come for a walk along the sand. Just as she did, she saw Carly crossing the street towards her.

"Eden, hi!" She smiled at Danny then turned

back to Eden. "I'm glad I got to see you. Grant told me not come over this morning before I went to work. He said we needed to back off and give you some space."

"Oh." So that explained it. *He* needed to back off and *he* needed some space after their discussion yesterday about his wife. Silly to feel disappointed again.

"He's right. I forget we can be a bit overwhelming at times."

"No, you're not overwhelming. You're all sweet."

"Yeah sure," Carly joked. She ruffled Danny's hair. "Now, we want you two to come to dinner tonight."

"Yippee!" Danny exclaimed.

Eden frowned as her heart thudded at the thought of seeing Grant. "Tonight?"

"You don't have other plans, do you?"

"I haven't been here long enough to have plans."

"Good." Carly glanced over at the store as a couple of people entered. "I'd better go and help Nancy. We'll see you at seven then."

Eden agreed as Carly walked away, but she wondered whether Grant knew about this. She wouldn't feel comfortable going for dinner if he didn't want her there.

"Hey, let's go to the garage," she said to Danny. "I've just remembered I need to speak to Grant about something."

"Yippee!" Danny said again and started racing ahead.

"Wait for me," she said, hurrying after him.

At the garage, Danny called out to Sean who was in the office looking like he was either writing or drawing. Her son dashed over to his friend. Grant had his head over the engine of a car, and there was no sight of Tom.

"Carly's invited us for dinner tonight," Eden said when she reached Grant.

He turned his head to look at her without expression, then back to the engine. "Fine."

"Oh." She waited for further response but there was nothing. "I just wanted to let you know."

"Why?" His head stayed down.

"Er... in case you had any objections."

He straightened then and looked at her in surprise. "Why would I have objections?"

"I just thought you might."

He shrugged, but this time his eyes turned blank. "You're a neighbour, that's all. I have no objections."

She winced inwardly, hurt but not sure why.

"Good." Sean and Danny came up to them. An idea occurred to her. "Oh by the way, Grant, would it be okay for Sean to come back with us?" she heard herself say, partly in retaliation for his indifference. She knew Sean and Danny would put pressure on Grant, which they did.

"Go on then," he told his son. He looked at Eden with sudden wry amusement. "Not fair."

"All's fair in —"

A speculative look entered his eyes. "Yes?"

She shrugged. "Well, you know the rest of the saying," she said breezily, then hurried away with the boys. There was certainly no love between her and Grant, but there was definitely some sort of internal war going on.

###

That evening as Eden walked across her backyard to the gap in the fence, Danny raced ahead of her, excited about playing with Sean again even though Sean had only gone home two hours ago. She was happy for her son. And a little excited herself, especially since giving Grant forewarning that she would be there.

"Danny, slow down," she said, trying not to feel self-conscious when she saw a few more people than expected sitting in the pergola area near the other side of the house.

"You didn't have to bring anything," Carly said, taking the cake that Eden had bought from the local bakery.

"I couldn't come without bringing something," Eden said.

"Of course you could," Carly said warmly. "You never have to bring anything when you come here. Just pop over any time."

Eden's gaze slid to Grant but as she met his eyes an odd excitement shot through her at the thought of seeing him *any time*. Quickly she looked back at Carly.

Just then a younger version of Grant got to his feet and held out his hand. "Hi, Eden. I'm Ryan."

She smiled. "Hi, Ryan."

"And I'm Jared," another version of Grant said, getting to his feet and offering his hand like his brother. Jared winked at Tom. "Hey, Dad, I might just have to move back home now you've got such a lovely neighbour."

"Yeah, me too," Ryan quipped.

Carly waved a dismissing hand at them in a sisterly fashion. "Ignore them."

Eden laughed, relaxing with them in spite of feeling a little self-conscious. She wasn't used to handsome men flirting with her. Then she looked at Grant and saw he wasn't smiling. He was staring at his brothers with a closed look.

"My sons are a bit too much at times," Tom said with a smile. "As Carly said, just ignore them."

Just then a little girl came up to them.

"This is Zoe," Carly said, picking up her daughter.

Eden smiled at the little sweetheart. So far, she'd only seen the little girl at a distance. "Hello, Zoe."

Zoe hid her face in her mother's neck.

"She doesn't take after her mother that's for sure," Ryan joked.

The tone was set for the evening. The two men flirted with Eden, but it was harmless. Nice but harmless. Yet for some odd reason it was like they were teasing her to get Grant to react.

Then after eating, Carly said, "Oh Eden, I almost forgot. Do you remember Amy from the restaurant? She was the waitress."

Eden thought a moment. "Yes."

"Well, she lives down the road and she asked me to ask you if you needed someone to look after Danny during the school holidays. She usually goes to school in the day but she's on holiday too right now."

Hope rose inside Eden. "So you're recommending her?" she asked, yet giving herself time to think about the offer. She had been worried about taking Danny with her on the job, especially being new and him having to be with her all day. He was a good kid, but he did get bored.

"Yes. She's responsible. She'll be going to university in a few months."

"I recommend her too," Tom said, and Jared

and Ryan added their recommendations as well.

Clearly Amy was a good choice. And Danny had seemed to like her. "Then I think I might take her up on that offer."

"Great," Carly said, looking pleased. "I'll speak to Amy tomorrow and get the ball rolling."

"Thanks so much, Carly," Eden said with sincerity.

Carly grinned. "Hey, I'll be doing myself a favour. I don't want Danny let loose in the store with all those gift packs of chocolates around. He'd eat my profits."

"They'd be probably too fancy for him," Eden joked right back, knowing Danny would eat any chocolate he could get his hands on if she let him.

The two women smiled at each other.

"Right," Grant suddenly said as if he'd had

enough of all this friendliness. "That's all sorted then."

His words hurt her a little. She wasn't sure why. She certainly hadn't expected any favour at all from him. And yet she knew that wasn't fair. After all, he had brought them lunch yesterday. He wasn't totally detached.

Just then the boys came racing over and Eden told Danny about Amy.

"Does it mean I can play with Sean every day?"

Eden's gaze shot to Grant. "Er... I'm not sure. Sean's still grounded and I'm only paying Amy to look after one of you."

"Oh, but Amy's nice," Sean said. "She'll look after me too." There was full confidence in his voice.

"You're still grounded," Grant said

somewhat firmly.

Sean looked a little deflated, but he shrugged and quickly raced off to play again. Clearly, he would work on his father when the time came.

"You realise they are going to make your life hell until you give in?" Ryan teased his brother.

"Blackmail doesn't fly with me." Grant's tone wasn't as tough as he was making out.

"They'll be good company for each other," Jared reflected.

"We'll see," was all Grant said, and somehow now she knew he would relent. There was a mellow look in his eyes that she was beginning to recognise.

A warm glow filled her as a sense of family surrounded her. And that was strange. She'd never felt so cossetted by so many people before. It really was a lovely, lovely feeling.

She let herself bask in the moment, but then put

it to the side as she saw Carly start to stack up the dirty plates, then Grant began to help too. Jared and Ryan had now started a discussion about a football game and didn't appear to notice.

Eden started to help.

"Leave them, Eden," Tom said, little Zoe sitting on his lap. "You're a guest here."

"No, it's fine, Tom," she dismissed with a smile. "I need to stretch my legs." But secretly she was still enjoying being part of their family and doing what families did together.

She helped Carly carry some of the dirty plates inside, aware of Grant following behind. The other woman was chatting away as she placed some items in the refrigerator, but Eden was only aware of Grant close by as he brushed past her and put some things on the sink. She didn't mean to, but she spun around too quickly, and heat shot through her veins as their eyes met. She hadn't expected him to be quite so close. Her breath caught high in her throat as suddenly she realised that Carly had headed back outside, and she was now alone with Grant.

Every instinct was telling her to move away. And conversely every instinct was telling her to stay. "Your family's so nice," she said, trying to put a mental distance between them at least.

Something flickered in his gorgeous blue eyes. "My brothers like to joke around."

"And you don't?"

"Sometimes," he muttered gruffly.

All at once his eyes took on a sensuality that made her heart skip a beat. She licked her suddenly dry lips. "Um... you're the serious one of the family, are you?"

"We're all serious when need be." Without warning his gaze dropped to her mouth. Before she could react, his head began to lower.

And lower still...

He placed his lips on hers.

A soft gasp rose in her throat as he stilled for a few heart-stopping seconds. Time itself stood still, the feel of his mouth against hers as if made to be there.

Then the sound of Tom's voice coming towards the kitchen cut through the moment and broke them apart. She managed to spin back to the sink and turn on the tap.

"Here you go, Grant," Tom said from behind them. "Make yourself useful and put these away for me. Eden, you're a guest. Just leave all that in the sink and come back outside."

She glanced over her shoulder, grateful that Tom didn't seem to realise something had just occurred between her and his son. "I don't mind,

Tom." Somehow she sounded normal.

He waved a dismissive hand. "No, I insist. Grant, bring our new neighbour outside and don't take no for an answer." His voice faded away as he disappeared out the door again.

Silence surrounded her and Grant.

"I'm sorry about that," he said, cutting through the silence.

She managed a shrug. "That's okay. Your dad was just being nice."

"I don't mean Dad. I meant I shouldn't have kissed you." His voice sounded gruff as if angry with himself.

An odd ache of pain shot through her. "Oh." Martin hadn't wanted to kiss her much either, though no man had ever apologised for it before. "It was only a kiss," she said, playing it down.

His brows drew together. "Only?"

She suspected he was merely assessing her reaction. "Let's not make any more of it than it was."

His eyes probed hers for a second more and she held her ground, then as if satisfied he nodded. "Fine." He picked up a clean tea towel and tossed it to her. "Now dry your hands, new neighbour. Dad will kill me if I don't get you back to the others soon." He was making a joke of it, his mouth curving slightly with an amusement that didn't fool her. Those eyes weren't amused. Not at all. He was still berating himself over that kiss.

He waved her ahead of him and she attempted a smile, but she had a deflated feeling in her stomach as she dried her hands. She headed for the door, aware of him right behind her, and told herself to put it into perspective. Okay, so he had apologised. No big deal. One kiss wasn't going to do too much damage in the scheme of things. All was well in her world, right?

If not in his.

###

Grant returned to the others, certainly not happy with himself. What the hell was he doing kissing Eden? And why the hell had she stood there and let him? He wasn't sure what had made him reach out like that and kiss her, but he knew he hadn't been able to stop himself.

Of course, he blamed his brothers for the kiss. Somehow they'd known he was attracted to Eden and had been determined to try and make him jealous. And it had worked, darn it! He'd wanted to tell them to stop being so childish. That games like this belonged to their teenage years. But it would have only made them tease him more.

And yet, if he was honest with himself, he had to admit it was more than that and this wasn't about his brothers at all. He'd been wanting to kiss her ever since he'd pulled up on the road leading into Opal Bay and saw her standing there beside her car, silently protecting her son. At that moment there had been something about her that had unknowingly slipped under his guard. Something warm and exciting deep inside of him. Something that felt so true. So genuine. It wasn't a feeling he had been familiar with in his marriage, so it shook him a little.

Yeah, that's all it was, he decided, pushing thoughts of Eden aside. No use trying to figure it out any further. Eden was merely a passing fancy in the scheme of things. He could handle that.

###

On Monday morning Eden left Danny with Amy and arrived at work fifteen minutes early. Last night Carly had offered to give her a ride to the shop, but Eden preferred to take her own car, not wanting either of them to be reliant upon the other. Besides, she liked being independent. She was used to it.

The morning was a little slow with customers at first and Eden was grateful for the chance to learn the ropes. The shop had an assortment of touristy knick-knacks plus some expensive items as well. There was a storage room at the back plus a tiny office. Carly said she would stay a day or two until Eden felt comfortable about doing this by herself. She also mentioned that a couple of tourist buses came to town on a Tuesday and Thursday as well as the weekends and that she usually helped then.

"And I've got a couple of local ladies who make the touristy stuff," Carly said, "and a couple of local men who make some of the wood pieces. I also get items from surrounding areas to sell on consignment."

The afternoon was much busier, being school holidays and summer.

"It's been a busy day," Carly said, when business started to slow around four in the afternoon. She carried a cup of coffee over to Eden. "Here we go. Take a break."

Eden felt exhausted but she wasn't about to say so. She just hoped she could get through another three days of this without collapsing. Once she got home and put her feet up, she'd be okay, she told herself as she sipped at her coffee.

"You look all-in," Carly said sympathetically.

Eden managed a smile. "I'm fine."

Carly shot her a knowing look. "I remember when I first opened the store five years ago. It took me a few weeks to get used to it. I used to drag myself home each night and cry because my feet ached so much. It slows down a little before Easter, then the winter tourists come. Thank goodness for them though."

"My feet *are* killing me," Eden admitted.

"Of course, that was nothing until I got pregnant," Carly joked. "Thankfully my brothers stepped in and got me some help before I killed myself."

Eden could easily see Jared and Ryan helping. "It's good to have brothers like that."

"Yeah, they were great about it all." She looked at Eden. "Someone's bound to tell you sooner or later about me. I fell for a smooth talker who left town as soon as he found out I was pregnant. I can't regret having Zoe though."

"We all get taken in by the wrong people at times," Eden sympathised, understanding totally.

"You too? I mean, I know you're divorced and all..."

Eden nodded.

Carly sent her a flash of sympathy then got to her feet. "Look, I have to pop over to the supermarket. I want you to just sit here and relax. Don't do anything else. I'll be back in time to lock up."

Eden took Carly's advice and relaxed for a while after she left, just letting herself soak up the atmosphere of the store while it was at its quietest. And then the front doorbell rang, and she looked up to see a woman coming through the door, and all too soon it was back to business.

The rest of the week was uneventful but busy and Eden was grateful for that. She finally felt like she was moving on in life. And her feet agreed!

Chapter Seven

"Can I go please, Mum?" Danny said, racing in the back door with Sean the following Saturday afternoon.

She smiled at the enthusiasm on their faces. "Go where, honey?"

"For a sleepover at Sean's place. Mister Ridgeway said I could."

Eden looked at Sean. "So you've asked your father and he said yes?" She knew they wouldn't lie to her, but she also knew how kids manipulated adults at times. And she didn't want to upset Grant, who'd been giving her a wide berth this past week. She'd been grateful for that. She'd had enough to contend with the new job without being aware of Grant and remembering that kiss.

No, she wasn't going to think about that kiss again.

No.

No way.

"My granddad said it was okay," Sean said, interrupting her thoughts. "We haven't asked my dad yet."

"Well, you'd better go ask him first," she said.

Just then, Tom knocked on the screen door then stepped inside. "It's okay, Eden," he said, obviously hearing the conversation. "Grant's fine with it. We all are."

"The boys might be too rowdy for Zoe," she pointed out.

Tom chuckled. "Probably the other way around," he said, and Eden laughed.

"Please, Mummy?" Danny begged like it was the most important thing in the world. And no doubt to him it was.

She looked at his eager little face and any objection dissolved. She knew he was manipulating her by calling her Mummy instead of Mum, but she would let him get away with it this time. He'd had so little male attention over the years from Martin. This would do him good.

She smiled. "Okay, you can go, honey."

"Yippee!" Danny said, and Sean whooped too. "Come on. Let's go get my things." He headed for his bedroom.

Eden wasn't sure what 'things' he wanted to take. "Hang on, young man. I'll come help." Her words trailed after him.

Tom laughed as he pushed open the screen door and stepped outside. "Send them over when you're ready."

"Will do. And thanks, Tom."

He stopped for a moment and glanced back at her, his eyes somehow understanding how much this meant to her and to Danny. "You're very welcome, Eden."

He left them to it and Eden hurried into Danny's bedroom to check on what he was putting in his backpack. She was a little excited for herself as well as Danny. It would be nice to have a night to herself.

###

Eden loved sitting on the verandah later that evening, sipping at a glass of wine, soft music from the radio playing in the background. Low illumination spilled out from the lamp in the loungeroom as she looked out over the bay, other lights bobbing like lanterns from a couple of boats out on the water. The scent of the ocean wafted up to her on a gentle summer breeze and she felt relaxed, knowing that Danny would be having a good time over at Sean's place next door.

She still couldn't believe her luck that things had fallen into place so quickly and so easily. Both Tom and Grant were so patient with the kids and that was comforting. After Martin, it was refreshing for men to be interested in what children had to say.

Just then the security light at the corner of the house came on and Grant suddenly appeared. He stopped at the bottom step when he saw her sitting on the verandah.

"Hi," he said, looking good in jeans and a t-shirt.

"Hi."

"I saw your light on and just thought I'd pop in to see how you are." He glanced at the wine in her hand. "I see you're okay," he said, relaxing into a slight smile that surprised her. After their kiss, she hadn't expected him to be relaxed around her at all. She definitely didn't feel quite as relaxed now that he was here.

She smiled back a little. "Just taking it easy."

"Good." He sounded like he meant it.

"Would you like a glass of wine? I don't have

anything else I'm afraid." She'd only bought the one bottle today, sometimes liking a glass in the evening.

"Yeah, that would be good."

She waved towards the other chair. "Sit down and I'll get you one."

He started up the couple of steps. "I can get it."

"No, it's okay." She got to her feet, needing a moment to herself. "I know where the glasses are."

"Okay."

Her hands were shaking a little as she poured the wine. Why oh why did he make her react like this? He attracted her on so many levels that she'd never felt before. But could it only be because she had never felt such a connection to a man like this before? Certainly, Martin had swept her off her feet. He'd been handsome and charming, and she'd thought he'd wanted her but now she knew he'd only been looking for something inside of himself that wasn't there. Unfortunately, she'd learned that far too late.

"Dad and Carly are looking after the boys," he said when she came back and handed him the glass.

"I didn't think you'd leave them by themselves," she teased, sitting down on the other chair and trying to keep things light.

"I had to go check on a friend's car. He needs it for Monday."

"Did you manage to fix it?"

He grimaced. "No, unfortunately. I had to take it back to the garage. I'll work on it in the morning."

"You're a good friend."

He shrugged. "That's what friends do."

"True. But I bet you'd even fix it for a stranger if they needed it in a hurry."

"Only if they paid me double," he said with a sudden grin that made her knees go weak.

Just as well she was already sitting down. "Oh, so that's where *I* went wrong."

His smile faded. "You could have paid me triple and I would still have needed that part."

"I know. And I also know you'd only charge what the job was worth no matter who it was."

"Thank you, Eden."

The intensity of his gaze melted something inside her, and she quickly looked down at her wine. "I hope the boys are behaving themselves."

"I doubt it," he joked, and she chuckled. For a moment there was silence, then, "Does Danny ever see his father?"

She looked up at him, taken by surprise by the question. "No. Not yet. It just causes too much heartache."

He inclined his head in understanding, but his eyes seemed to focus in on her. "Are you still in love with your husband?"

She felt herself gasp a little. "That's a very personal question."

"I know." He didn't apologise.

She gave herself a second to think, and somehow found she didn't mind answering. "My *ex*-husband, you mean? No. I don't think I was ever in love with Martin." She hesitated, not sure how much to say but decided she wanted to share this with Grant. She automatically knew he wasn't one to gossip. "You see, I was young and thought I was in love, but it was just infatuation. I fell pregnant before I realised the difference. But our marriage was a mistake. A mistake I was willing to live with for the sake of Danny."

His eyes acknowledged her comment.

"Unfortunately, Martin wasn't ready for marriage or fatherhood." Her lips tightened. "He certainly wasn't prepared to put Danny first when he ran off and left us." No, Martin had been too concerned with himself and hadn't really been interested in anything Danny said or did.

"Maybe he was doing you and Danny a favour by leaving?"

"Absolutely." Her heart cramped. "It was just the way he did it. He should have asked me for a divorce first rather than be unfaithful."

"True. That would have been the right thing to do."

"Of course, now I worry that Danny might hold this against me in years to come. Not letting him see his dad, that is."

"If your ex wanted to see Danny, would you let him?"

She'd already prepared herself that this may eventuate. "As hard as it would be for me, yes."

"Then you're doing the right thing." After a moment his gaze dropped to his glass, and he swirled the wine a little. "I worried if I was doing the right thing by Sean, you know," he said, as if talking to the glass. "Once Eve and I separated, I wasn't sure whether to stay in contact with him or not. I didn't want to make it harder for him but in the end I couldn't stop myself." He looked up at her. "I needed him in my life. It was that simple."

His words touched her. "He clearly needed you too."

Their eyes met in a mutual bonding that felt too good.

She forced herself to think beyond the moment. "Martin isn't like you, Grant. He never cared about his son."

"That's a shame."

"He was a token father and that's all. Until we came here, and I met you and your family, I didn't understand that. My own father died when I was young, and my mother never remarried so I didn't have any father figures in my life." She realised what she'd said. "Oh, I didn't mean to imply I'm looking for another father for Danny."

The corners of his mouth quirked a little. "I know that."

Her heart turned over at the caring in this man. He was so different to Martin. All at once she heard herself saying, "Martin was a womaniser, you see." The words spilled from her mouth. "He was always having affairs."

Grant's head snapped back. "*What?*"

She bit her lip, seeing the shock in his eyes. "I'm sorry. I shouldn't have said anything. Please forget what I said."

The words hung in the air.

"That's a little hard to forget," he muttered.

She cleared her throat. "Yes, I know." Boy oh boy, did she know that.

A couple of seconds ticked by, then Grant spoke, "So *he was unfaithful?*"

She nodded. "Frequently. Only, I didn't know about it for a long time. Not until I found him in bed with someone he said he fell in love with."

He let out a slow breath. "That's really tough on you."

"It was." She appreciated his kindness.

"Was?"

"I'm over it. I mean I'm over Martin." Her lips tightened. "I'm not so forgiving over what it did to Danny and me."

"I don't blame you," he said gruffly. "I'm sorry

he hurt you like that."

She took a shaky breath. "Thank you."

"Does Danny know?"

"No, thank goodness," she said with relief. "No doubt he will learn about it in time but he's only a little boy. I don't want him growing up too quickly."

"For sure."

Suddenly she didn't want to think about the future. And she didn't want to think about the past either. The here and now was what was important, she reminded herself, as she tried to relax as the soft music from the radio floated out from the lounge room and the summery night air brushed past her. Sitting here on her verandah, sipping wine with a friend — and yes, she considered Grant a friend now — is what really mattered.

"I love this song," she said to settle her

bouncing thoughts and to calm herself even more. The music was a slow, dreamy, romantic song that always made her feel... well... dreamy.

A moment crept by then Grant pushed to his feet. "Dance with me," he said, holding out his hand.

Her stomach fluttered. "What? Here?"

"Why not?"

She tried to gather her thoughts, but her mind suddenly didn't seem to be working properly. She wasn't sure it was a good idea. Not when she was beginning to feel... well... dreamy.

What to do?

She looked at his hand, then looked back up to his face. It was a face she could trust. She knew that now with certainty.

She reached out and put her hand in his. He pulled her up close, but he didn't quite press her against him, and one part of her was disappointed, another relieved. Just being this close was shooting desire through her. She wasn't used to such a feeling.

He smelt good too.

Too?

Yeah, he *smelt* good and he *felt* good.

And oh, he *looked* so very, very good.

In the muted light, his gaze intensified on her. Then slowly he drew her an inch closer and started moving her in a slow dance. Something more flickered in those eyes, and a tingle skittered along her skin.

"So you like this?" he murmured, his warm, pleasant breath wafting over her.

"Wh...what?"

"The song."

She licked her lips, not used to the intimate

touch of his body against hers. "Yes."

"You're a romantic, then?"

"Um... not really."

"Me either."

Why did she feel disappointed?

"Though..." he added, "I *do* know how to be romantic when the time calls for it."

Her heart began dancing around like a puppet on a string. "And when is that?" she asked for something to say.

"I think the time calls for it right now," he murmured.

He didn't give her any further time to think. He lowered his head and kissed her. Only, this kiss wasn't merely his lips on hers like their last kiss. This time his tongue immediately sought her out and he kissed her in a long, slow kiss. Her legs turned to jelly, and she began to melt against him.

My oh my, this man knew how to kiss.

Eventually he eased back, his eyes closing in on her. "I want to make love to you, Eden."

The breath stalled in her throat and all she could manage was an, "Oh."

This was the last thing she expected him to say. She tried to think. Going from a kiss to her bed was a huge jump. A leap of faith really. Her head whirled as she tried to think. And yet he wasn't asking or taking. He was merely stating a fact. Was she ready to take this leap of faith?

Yes, she decided, she was. Just like she'd taken a leap of faith staying here in this town. This was the next step for her. And she had to admit she wanted something to take away with her when she finally left here. The thought of leaving sealed it.

"I want that too," she said softly.

Tiny flames seemed to leap in his blue eyes,

and he gave a low groan.

His kisses led her all the way to the bedroom. Then time disappeared. She could feel the heat of his hands as they stroked their way down her body, feeling her, getting to know her as he stripped her clothes away. With shaking hands, she did the same to him. He made love to her in a way she'd never known before, raising all her senses to high alert, gentle and incredibly attentive. It was the most amazing experience she'd ever known.

Afterwards, as she lay in the crook of his arm, it took her a moment to realise a tear was slipping down her cheek. She quickly brushed the wetness aside, but Grant saw and he was immediately concerned.

He went up on one selbow. "You're crying."

"I didn't mean to."

"Did I hurt you?"

"No, of course not. You were wonderful and caring." Her throat tightened with emotion. "And you wanted me."

He arched a brow. "What's so surprising about that?"

"No, I mean, you *really* wanted me. You see, I've only ever made love with Martin before now."

"Oh sweetheart," he said brusquely.

"I somehow knew the sex wasn't memorable with him, but you made me see how great it can be." Emotion swelled inside her. "I was ashamed that I never really seemed enough for him, you see. I thought it was my own fault. When I found out about his affairs I realised no one woman would be enough for him."

"You have nothing to be ashamed about, Eden." He lay back down and pulled her close, resting the side of her face against his bare chest. "Nothing," he reiterated, kissing the top of her head. "And you're more than enough for any man."

She relaxed against him. "Thank you," she whispered.

"No need to thank me for anything," he rasped.

His caring enveloped her like nothing she'd ever known. She placed her palm against his chest, loving the warmth of his skin, the warmth of the man himself. They lay like that for a while, then, "Make love to me again, Grant."

Without a word he eased her onto her back and swept her along a wave of desire that peeled back all thought, leaving her exposed to him in more ways than one. As they climaxed together, he looked deeply into her eyes. She had nowhere to hide, and she didn't care. They were one together and that was more than any moment she'd ever had with her ex-husband.

She fell asleep in his arms.

Eventually a movement in the room woke her. "Are you leaving?" she said, going up on one arm as he stood beside the bed and pulled on his jeans.

"Yes. It's three in the morning." He smiled gently down at her. "I need to protect your reputation."

"Grant, about all this..."

"Sssh, we'll talk another time."

"But –" She wasn't sure what she wanted to say yet.

"Go back to sleep, sweetheart."

"But –"

"You're going to be exhausted tomorrow if you don't get some sleep and so am I. And those boys of ours won't let us rest, you know."

He made it sound like they were a family, but she knew he didn't mean it like that.

He gave her a quick kiss. "Now go to sleep." He started towards the door.

"Yes, sir."

"I'm glad you know who's boss around here," he teased over his shoulder.

"Yeah. Your father." Smiling, she heard his soft snicker as he left the bedroom, flicking off the loungeroom lamp as he went and plunging the house into darkness.

But as she lay there in the dark, she had to wonder what would change now that they had taken this step. It wasn't so much her own reputation she was worrying about. It was how it would affect Danny if others knew. She finally came to the conclusion that what happened between her and

Grant had to be a one-off thing and was to be kept private between the two of them. Surely Grant would agree? After all, he had his own son to protect.

###

Grant silently cut across the backyard, careful to sneak into the darkened house. Not that he cared about himself. Call him old-fashioned but he really didn't want Eden's reputation to suffer if anyone saw him cutting across the grass between the houses. And he certainly didn't want to be caught out by the boys, not that they would have understood what had occurred.

Thankfully, all was quiet as he fell into bed. For a short while, he couldn't sleep, his mind churning over everything now he had time to actually think about things. He'd been humbled by Eden's confession that she'd been moved by him wanting her. *Of course,* he'd wanted her. He'd wanted her from the moment he'd laid eyes on her. *Damn her ex.*

Anger began to boil inside him. How could that bastard have left her such a terrible legacy? Eden was a generous lover and had deserved better than to be married to a man who'd cheated on her like Martin had. The man should have had the decency to respect his wife and child and give them their freedom, as hard as that would have been for them. It had been selfish of this Martin to stay. Selfish of him to allow Eden to believe she wasn't enough for him when in actual fact he'd had his own agenda.

Grant was glad he'd been able to show her how making love should be between two people who admired and respected each other. In a way, it was a new feeling for him too. Oh, he'd always respected the women he'd gone to bed with, but with Eden it had seemed richer somehow. More intense. More... feeling.

That thought was sudden and disconcerting, so he quickly rolled over onto his side to get some sleep. He definitely needed some shuteye. He wasn't exactly sure what their next step would be. Not sure he could be around Eden and not make love to her. On the other hand, he didn't want her to feel used. One thing was certain. They would have to talk.

Thankfully Grant caught up on some Sunday

morning sleep before going to the garage, but his brain still stumbled over all that had happened to Eden, not to mention all that had happened *between* him and Eden. He knew he had to speak to her as soon as he could, but he was rather relieved he had a bit of time to himself to think things over. God, how things had changed in the space of a night.

"Excuse me, buddy," a male voice said at the door to the garage office. "Can you tell me where I'd find Eden Beresford?"

Grant's head snapped up as unease rippled through him. "And you are?" he said, but he knew. *Oh yes, he knew.*

"Her husband."

Grant stiffened. "Her *ex-husband*, I believe."

There was a pause and the other man's eyes turned cold. "That's none of your business. Now, are you going to tell me, or do I have to ask somewhere else?"

Grant knew he had to let Eden know the guy was here. "She's gone into Port Macquarie for a few hours," he lied, hoping to buy her some time.

"You seem to know a lot about my wife's whereabouts."

"Your *ex-wife*, you mean?" he said before he could stop himself, then saw the speculatively look in the other man's eyes. Grant forced himself to shrug like he couldn't care less anyway. "Everyone knows everyone else around here. Besides, my sister has gone with her. That's how I know where she is."

The other man held his gaze for a moment then seemed to accept that. "A few hours, you say?" He started to turn away. "I can wait."

"Try the pub down the road. It's cooler in there," Grant said, wanting to get the guy out of the way.

The ex nodded then turned on his heels and left.

Grant waited until the other man's car drove off, then he hurriedly shut up the garage and drove to Eden's house. She was sitting on the back verandah, looking out over the bay.

Eden's heart raced when she saw Grant come around the side of the house. He had the look of a man on a mission. She knew they had to talk but she wasn't sure she was quite ready yet.

"Grant, what are you doing here?" she said, trying to sound calm. All at once she noticed the look on his face. She froze. "Something's the matter? What is it?"

"Where's Danny?" he said straight off.

For no good reason her heart squeezed inside her chest. "He's still over at your place with Sean and your Dad. Why?"

"Your ex is here."

Eden jumped to her feet. "What!"

"I told him you'd gone into Port Macquarie with Carly and wouldn't be back for a few hours. I wanted time to get back here and warn you."

"He's got a nerve," Eden said, but she was in panic, her mind trying to take it in. Martin was here in Opal Bay? There was only one reason. She knew he didn't want to see *her*. "He wants to see Danny," she muttered with a growing sense of despair. Who had given her away? Her mother? No. Her aunt was more a sucker for a sob story.

"So this is where you are," a male voice said.

"Martin!" she gasped, looking past Grant at the man who'd come around the side of the house.

He stopped and smirked at Grant. "I knew you'd lead me to her. You've got it bad, mate, haven't you?"

"Shut up," Grant warned.

Eden quickly tried to gather her thoughts. She drew herself up straighter. "What do you want, Martin?"

"To see my son."

She dare not let him see her reaction just yet. "Why? You weren't much interested in him before."

"I was unhappy."

"With me."

"Yes. But not now." He hesitated. "Now I want my family back," he said, shocking her. "You and Danny."

"Good grief!" She shuddered.

"I made a mistake with Paula. It wasn't love."

Her lips twisted. "She dumped you, did she?"

Martin winced, then lifted his chin in a way she

knew well when he was in the wrong. "Kind of. But that's not why I'm here. I love you, Eden, and I know I did wrong but I'm hoping we can start again."

She stood there looking at him. She just couldn't believe that after all he'd put her through, he would even think she would go back to him. She only had to remember finding him in bed with Paula, not to mention the aftermath. And what about all the other affairs he'd thrown up at her when he'd tried to blame her for his adultery? Oh God. *No*!

"You have a damn cheek coming here and saying that to me," she growled.

"I love you, Eden. I really do. And Danny, of course."

"You call that love? You didn't think about me or Danny when you hopped into bed with Paula. Hell, Martin! If it hadn't been me who caught you, one day it could have been our *son*.”

He stood there looking quite helpless, but she knew it was an act. He was just plain pathetic. “Eden, what can I say?”

“Nothing, Martin. There’s nothing more to say. I told you before that if you want to see your son, you will have to go through my lawyer.” She wasn’t sure if she could stop him but she’d give it her absolute best try.

“A man can change.”

“A man can *pretend* to change.”

“I’ll fight you on this.”

“Do your worst, Martin.” Her lips twisted. “Oh, that’s right. You’ve already done that.”

His mouth tightened then purposely relaxed. “Eden, look—”

“And now you’d better leave. I’d hate to think of you staying here in town overnight and tainting us with your presence."

"That's enough, Eden," he snapped. "I'll leave town when I'm —"

"Grant!"

They all spun towards the voice and saw Carly running towards them through a gap in the fence. Something else was obviously wrong.

"What's the matter, Carly?" Grant said.

Carly reached them and took a breath. "I was standing at my bedroom window rocking Zoe to sleep..." She sucked in another breath. "I saw the tail end of Sean and Danny heading into the bush down the end of the road."

Grant swore.

Eden's heart lurched in her chest. "What! Danny knows not to leave the house. Why would he do such a thing?" She felt the blood drain from her face as she spun towards Martin who was coming slowly towards them. "Oh God, Danny couldn't have heard us talking, could he?"

"It doesn't matter if he did," Martin said without emotion. "It's time he learned the facts of life."

Grant took a few steps and grabbed him by the throat. "He's eight years old, Bozo. He shouldn't have to learn his father is a womaniser."

"Let me go."

Grant roughly let him go with a gesture of repugnance.

"There's more," Carly said, her eyes wide, her face white as she looked at her brother. "There's a bushfire started up."

"What! Where?"

"It's a fair distance away and not coming in this direction. Not unless..."

Eden swallowed. "Unless?"

"The wind changes," Grant rasped. "Bloody hell!" Grant looked at his sister. "Carly, go back home and call Ryan and Jared and tell them to stand by just in case. I think the boys will be headed to Flinders Creek."

"Dad's already calling them."

"Where's Flinders Creek?" Eden asked.

"Just down the road. Not far," he said soothingly but she could see his worried frown.

"Carly, you'd better get back to Dad and Zoe."

The mention of the creek made Eden feel sick. "I'm coming with you."

He shook his head. "You should stay here in case they come back."

"No, Grant. That's my son out there too."

He nodded. "Okay, let's take your car. It will be quicker."

"I'll just get my keys." She spun around to

head towards the verandah, and saw Martin whom she'd forgotten about. He seemed frozen to the spot. "Are you coming to look for your son?"

His gaze shifted away briefly. "No, I —" His mobile phone rang, and he looked almost relieved. "You go ahead. I'll meet you there."

Eden didn't have time to feel anything but disgust.

"Paula!" she heard her ex say with delightful surprise, and she and Grant exchanged a look of pure revulsion. Martin's son could be in danger and all he could think about was his lover.

Then thoughts of Danny came rushing back and she hurried inside and grabbed her car keys. They left Martin talking on the phone. She hoped to God he wasn't here when they returned, but right now that didn't matter. Right now the only important thing was that the boys be found safe and sound.

Chapter Eight

Grant felt swallowed up with fear as he ran around the side of the house, Eden hurrying beside him. After the swiftness of his ex-wife's death in that car accident, he knew firsthand how quickly life could change. Oh God, he didn't want to think about losing his son. He had to concentrate on finding Sean and Danny, though the sight of smoke from the bushfire a long way in the distance didn't ease his mind.

Hearing Eden's hurried breathing beside him, compassion rose in him for what she was going through. Compassion and an odd feeling of pain for her distress. He knew exactly how she felt. She would be anguished over what could happen to her son. Exactly the same as his own thoughts over what could happen to Sean. It didn't bear thinking about, yet they were both thinking it.

They were quiet as he drove towards the creek. If they'd stayed on the dirt road, the boys couldn't have gone too far.

And if they hadn't?

No, one thing at a time.

Then, "They wouldn't go near the water, would they?" Eden whispered as if she couldn't hold her panic in any longer. "What if they —"

And there they were.

"They're okay," he said, heaving a sigh of the greatest relief as he pointed them out ahead. Both boys were sitting under a tree by the edge of the creek, throwing stones in the water. If he hadn't been driving, Grant would have kissed the ground. Or kissed Eden.

"Thank God!" Eden exclaimed in a shaky voice.

"Yes."

"If anything had happened to Danny ..."

"I know."

She spun towards Grant. "Sean too," she added.

He knew she meant it and at that moment something crystallised inside him. Something so intense it blurred their current situation with the boys for the softest of seconds. And for the first time ever he toppled headlong in love. For the first time ever, he fully comprehended what loving a woman was really all about.

The boys got to their feet when they saw the car, and Eden felt the tears well in her eyes as she jumped out of the passenger side and raced towards them. Thank you, God! She couldn't have borne it if anything had happened to her son.

She grabbed Danny and hugged him to her. He was so precious. So very, very precious.

Once satisfied that he was okay, she pulled back and scolded him. "Danny, I told you not to leave the house. I was so worried."

His bottom lip began to tremble. "I saw Dad talking to you. I didn't want to see him."

So, he hadn't heard them talking? Intense relief raced through her. "Oh Danny."

Suddenly he threw his arms around her neck. "I don't want to go home, Mummy. I don't want Dad to take me away from here. I want to stay here with you."

She held him tight. "Oh honey, he's not going to take you anywhere," she murmured in his ear. Danny needed her as much as she needed him.

He pulled back and looked into her face. "Promise?"

Her heart swelled with maternal love for her child. "Yes, I promise. We're staying right here for now."

"Oh Mummy, thank you."

How bittersweet the moment. She was happy to make such a promise yet it pained her to have to make it in the first place.

"Mummy, I want to stay here *forever*."

Eden bit her lip. How could she say she

couldn't make such a promise?

All at once she became aware of Grant talking to Sean.

"Son, you know you shouldn't have gone into the bush."

"Yeah, I know, Dad, but I couldn't let Danny go by himself. He doesn't know the area."

Her eyes met Grant's. She felt terrible for inadvertently putting his son in danger like this. She'd meant it when she'd told Grant she'd be devastated if anything had happened to Sean as well as Danny.

Grant looked back at his son. "I'm proud of you for being such a good friend, Sean, but you should have told an adult."

"But Danny would have gone by himself."

Again, Grant's eyes met hers. How could they argue with such logic?

"We'll talk about this later. Come on, let's all go home."

Home.

Such a simple but meaningful word. With Martin, she'd never really had a home, as much as she'd tried. Actually, she'd never really *felt* at home with Martin either.

Yet with Grant saying that one word – *home* – she experienced a swelling of heartfelt emotion like she'd never known. It warmed her through. It filled her up. It felt so perfect, as if all her dreams and hopes had aligned with the universe. And she knew. Home wasn't really a place. It was a feeling. And for some reason, it had everything to do with Grant.

Before they drove off, Grant called his brothers on his mobile phone, then his father, to tell them the good news that the boys had been found safe and sound. It was decided that everyone would meet at the Ridgeway's house for Sunday brunch, though Eden suspected it more a matter of the family getting together after the fright they'd all had. Once again it showed the importance of having family. Of being at *home* with family.

Eden pushed aside any thoughts about that and what it all might mean as he turned off the dirt road and they headed back. She was so thankful the boys were alive and well, but there might still be another hurdle to face. Had Martin actually left?

She must have stiffened because Grant reached over and squeezed her hand as if he knew what she was thinking. She gave him a weak smile in appreciation. He was such a good man.

Mercifully, there was no sign of another car at her house, so she prayed that Martin had gone for good. She suspected he had but with Martin one never knew. What she *did* know was that she would protect her son in whatever way she could, come hell or high water.

Tom, Carly and Zoe were outside waiting for them when they drew up in Eden's driveway. There was some light scolding as well as some big hugs for the boys.

Carly leaned towards Eden and whispered, "He's gone, Eden."

Eden felt the tension seep out of her, and she nodded her thanks to Carly for letting her know, noting that Grant had seen the interaction.

"Now," Tom said, "everyone over to our place for pancakes. Jared and Ryan will join us soon."

Eden saw Danny hesitate. "You go, honey.

Your dad's not here." The visible relief on her son's face pulled at her heartstrings. "I'll just pop inside and drop off my car keys," she said, but she really wanted to look around to make sure Martin hadn't gone without leaving any nasty notes or reminders of him.

"I'll come with you, Eden," Grant said casually, but the look in his eyes said he wasn't letting her go alone. "Off you go, boys. We'll be over shortly. Save some pancakes for us," he joked, and the boys whooped and ran off with the others following them.

Once again, she was aware of Grant's kind nature. "I'm okay if you want to go with them."

"I'm coming with you."

His protectiveness warmed her. "Thank you." She started walking down the driveway to the back of the house and he fell into step beside her. They didn't talk as they climbed the steps to the verandah and went inside. Eden's gaze searched all over, and she was sure Grant's did too. Everything seemed in its place.

"All good?" Grant asked as she came out of her bedroom and into the lounge room where he was standing. She was glad he hadn't followed her in there, not when they still needed to discuss things between them. Heavens, was it only last night that they made love? So much seemed to have happened since then.

She nodded. "All good." Was he thinking the same as her? How they had lain together... joined together... back there in her bedroom. "I'm sorry that my personal problems impacted on you and Sean," she said quickly in case he wanted to discuss last night.

His eyes said he knew what she was thinking.

"It's not your fault, Eden."

"But it could have ended badly."

"It didn't."

"I know but—"

"Marry me."

Her breath caught. "Wh... what?"

He walked over to her and looped his arms around her waist. "I've fallen in love with you, Eden. Marry me."

She struggled to think. "You can't have... I mean, you can't know that."

"I can, and I do know." The look in his eyes was so steady, as if he knew for sure.

"But... but..." She fought to think. How could this be true? Things like this didn't happen in real life. Not to her. "Is this for Danny's sake?"

He blinked. "No, of course not. Why would you ask that?"

"So you can protect him from his father." It was just the type of thing he'd do.

"No need. You've done a good job of that so far," he said, sending warmth through her. "Look, okay yes, in a way this is about Danny but it's so much more. This is about you and me, Eden. Danny is a part of you, and I love you therefore he's now a part of me. I love him too."

A lump formed in her throat. "That's so sweet," she said huskily.

"It's the truth. It's how I feel." Another pause. "But I don't want you to marry me just for Danny's sake. I want you to marry me because you might come to love me too."

"I already do," she said before she could stop herself.

And everything in her life fell into place in that one moment.

His eyes flared. His arms tightened around her.

She realised she'd said exactly what was in her heart. "I've fallen in love with you too, Grant."

He brought his hands up to cup her face. "Oh sweetheart," he murmured, then kissed her, caressing her with his lips, his tongue taking long moments to brush hers with the taste of love.

When the kiss ended, he tenderly ran a fingertip down her cheek. "Sweetheart, we may have only known each other a short while, but our love is very real. I can feel it in every cell of my body."

His words filled her with joy. "I feel that too. With every pulse of my heart."

"It was meant to be, Eden. You and me."

She nodded. "I've never been more certain in my life... darling," she added, loving the sound of the endearment on her lips. Loving the freedom to say it.

He placed his warm lips against hers in a short but powerful kiss. Then, "Should we go tell our sons the good news?"

Eden couldn't help but smile with sheer happiness. "They'll be over the moon."

"So will my family."

At the mention of family, her happiness dimmed a little.

"What's wrong?"

"I'm not so sure about my mother. She may be a bit upset that we won't be coming back to Perth." Probably more than a bit upset. "She'll be here in a day or two."

He raised a brow. "How do you know that?"

"I know my mother. She'll want to check you out."

"I wouldn't expect anything less. But she's only going to find that I love you and Danny with all my heart." His expression softened even more. "Besides, she's not losing a daughter. She's gaining a son-in-law. And another grandson. I'd say it's a win-win situation, don't you?"

Eden looked at the man she loved, and the image of Sean came to mind. "Absolutely." Her doubts evaporated like a drop of water in the sun. "Actually, once she sees how much I love you, she'll fall in love with you too, and your family."

"Perhaps she'll want to move here to be near you?"

She had to smile. "You haven't met her yet."

"If you're her daughter then I know I'm going to like her."

Eden's heart swelled with love. She was so thankful she'd needed to take the turnoff to Opal Bay that day. Who would ever have thought where it would lead?

Another brief kiss, then he said, "Come on. Let's go before all the pancakes are gone."

"It doesn't matter. We can live off love," she teased.

They both smiled then their eyes locked on each other for a few seconds more, just as their hearts would always be locked on the other. And they both knew that this road to love had been a very special journey indeed.

THE END

About the Author

USA TODAY Bestselling Author, Maxine Sullivan, credits her mother for her love of romance novels, so it was natural for her to want to write them. This led to over 20 years of submitting stories and never giving up her dream of being published. That dream came true in 2006 when Maxine sold her first book to Harper Collins (Harlequin Desire line). Since that time, she has had 12 romance books published and has sold over 2 million copies worldwide in as many as 20 languages. Maxine is also published in short stories worldwide in national magazines like Woman's Day, New Idea, My Weekly, and has sold short stories to the True Confession magazines. She can be contacted through her website:

http://www.maxinesullivan.com

Other books

His Island Bride

Australian Millionaires:

The Millionaire's Seductive Revenge

The Tycoon's Blackmailed Mistress

The Executive's Vengeful Seduction

Diamonds Down Under:

Mistress & A Million Dollars

Valente:

The CEO Takes A Wife

The C.O.O. Must Marry

Valente's Baby

Billionaires and Babies:

His Ring, Her Baby

High-Society:

High-Society Secret Baby

High-Society Seduction

Dynasties: The Jarrods

Taming Her Billionaire Boss

Billionaires and Babies:

Secret Son, Convenient Wife